Glimmer

Glimmer

Annie Waters

G. P. Putnam's Sons / New York

Published by G. P. Putnam's Sons
Publishers Since 1838
a member of
Penguin Putnam Inc.
200 Madison Avenue
New York, NY 10016
Published simultaneously in Canada

The text of this book is set in Berling.
Book design by Chris Welch

Library of Congress Cataloging-in-Publication Data

Waters, Annie.
Glimmer / Annie Waters.
p.   cm.
ISBN 0-399-14254-1 (alk. paper)
I. Title.
PS3573.A815G58   1997   96-39465 CIP
813'.54—dc21

Printed in the United States of America
1   2   3   4   5   6   7   8   9   10

This book is printed on acid-free paper. ∞

I have been very lucky in Laura Gaines, as both editor and friend, in my little sisters and my funny brother, lost downtown on a street-car, wondering which way is home, and in Sam, my writing pal for life.

To M.S., instructor in catharsis

. . . the sense of what is real, the thought if
after all it should prove unreal,
The doubts of day-time and the doubts of
night-time, the curious whether and how,
Whether that which appears so is so, or is it
all flashes and specks?

Walt Whitman,
"There Was a Child Went Forth"

Glimmer

Chapter One

In the pea-thick heat of Indian summer, I lie naked on top of the comforter, my ankles outlined yellow by the moonlight that floods the narrow window beside my bed. I hold my breath, listening to hear beyond my own heartbeat—the shrill sound of a siren in the distance, of voices on the street below my window, of soft footsteps on the floor above me. Down the corridor from my room, music is playing.

But I am listening for the sound of someone present just outside my door. The door is locked, my dresser pushed up against it. The clock beside my bed says just after two a.m.

In four hours, my mother in St. Louis will be dressing for rounds at Barnes Hospital, where she is head of Pediatric Cardiology. At six, I'll call her.

"Darling," she'll say when I tell her what's the matter. "If he won't leave, call the police."

"I can't exactly call the police, Mama," I'll say to her without an explanation.

"But you can't lock yourself in your room all day," she'll say in the steady reassuring voice I remember from childhood.

"Thank you, Mama," I'll say to her. "I'll figure out something to do about it."

I don't end these conversations with "I love you," as the roommates I had when I arrived here for orientation four weeks ago are fond of doing.

"Love you," they tell their mothers, rolling their eyes, and then, hanging up the phone, catching a glimpse of themselves in the mirror, sucking in their cheeks for the maximum show of bones, they add, "Gawd, she drives me crazy."

My mother doesn't drive me crazy.

He is leaning against the door now. I can hear his breath, and it seems to me he's saying my name.

He knows my name. I told it to him this summer on Martha's Vineyard, where I went to wait tables because my older sister Emmy said that I should have a normal, late-adolescent sort of job before I went off to college in Connecticut, instead of working in my mother's office in St. Louis.

"Age-appropriate," according to my aunt Winona, who is a perfectly decent woman ruined by social work school.

So at my summer job in a resort community in the northeastern United States, I met a man who said that his name was Steven Carney and that he was twenty-eight and had just graduated from law school.

I knew he was lying.

I'm a person in whom other people confide. My sister Caroline tells me it's because I have the heart of an angel, but I, for one, know that whatever the origin of my heart, the real reason people trust me is that I'm fat.

"You're not fat," Caroline tells me. "You have medium bones."

I don't know what it means to have medium bones, and neither does Caroline, since she was born with the bones of a hummingbird. But I do know what it means to be fat.

When I look in the mirror, the woman I see has hips that spread beyond the mirror's capacity to reflect—larger than the hips of anyone I have ever met. So you can imagine what a pleasure it was for me to arrive here as a freshman pre-medical student and discover that, without exception, every woman at this particular university is bone-thin and beautiful.

The last place I saw Steven Carney was on the ferry from Martha's Vineyard to Woods Hole, and he was with a woman. I sat on a wooden bench on the deck with my head down, pretending to read *Middlemarch*, which is what I do in public places, and he sat down beside me, pressing his broad shoulder against me, whispering, "Hello, lovely Sage," with his cigarette breath in my ear. "I wish you'd give me your address so I could come see you."

"I don't know my address," I said, although the university had sent me the address as well as the information that Nancy Kedrick from New Haven, Connecticut, would be my roommate. Which turned out to be true until the third night of orientation, when Nancy found an empty bed in another room, packed up her clothes, her CD player, her brand-new Apple computer, her Trek bike, a stack

of self-portraits in plexiglass frames, a baggie of cocaine, and piles of CDs, and moved into a suite
downstairs with three young women with long silky
hair the color of saffron, who wear platform shoes
and tiny flower dresses that fall just to the cups of
their small bottoms.

"You don't mind, do you, Sage?" Nancy said in a
cheery voice, lugging her wardrobe to the elevator.
"You told me you liked to live alone, so I fig-
ured . . ." She shrugged.

"I love it alone," I agreed. What else could I say?

"Come have dinner with us t'night," she said,
taking the last of her possessions from our room.

"Sure."

"Meet us about six in the rap," she said.

But at six I wasn't hungry for dinner.

Steven Carney got off the ferry first. He waved
good-bye and got into the shuttle bus to Falmouth,
and I was met at the dock by Emmy and my
brother Jacob, who's a medical student at Washington University in St. Louis, and my second sister,
Caroline, who graduated from Rhode Island School
of Design with a degree in graphic arts and lives in
Philadelphia with my brother Tobias, who dropped
out of school a year ago in December and spends
the mornings on Caroline's futon smoking weed.

They had all come to meet me in Woods Hole, quite out of their way and on a Saturday, to take me to college. That is the kind of family we have.

Emmy asked who the guy was who waved and I said Steve Carney and Jacob asked should he kill him and I said there was nothing whatever between us to kill him for.

Which was a lie. There was something between us, but it's difficult to explain, because it wasn't the usual something you expect between a man and a woman.

From the beginning, I was afraid of Steven Carney. When I saw him, my blood thinned and I had trouble catching my breath.

"*Now, Sage,*" Mama's sister Winona said to me in late June at her rose garden of an office in downtown St. Louis. "You *don't* have to tell me, of course, but I have *only* your interest in mind. If you are sexually active, I *hope* you are *protected.*"

"I'm not sexually active," I told her.

I probably would have said that in any case, but as it is, I'm a peripheral member of a sexually inactive generation in spite of news in the press and media to the contrary.

Aunt Winona could barely believe her ears. After all, Emmy was pregnant at twenty, and Caroline—I won't even begin on the subject of Caroline.

"Are you sure, Sage?"

As if that sort of activity were something you forget.

"Quite sure," I said.

But I wanted to give her a sense of importance. "A feeling of worth" is how she would describe it. I was certain she had pamphlets on the subject and a list of gynecologists with notes written beside each of their names like "the best" or "very sensitive to women's issues" or "the dregs."

So I said, "But I will be."

It would have taken me weeks to read the amount of material necessary from Aunt Winona's point of view for a sexually active life. When I got home from her office, I simply tossed the pamphlets in the trash bin outside our house and went upstairs to my room.

The subject of my sexual activity came up again with my sisters the night before I started college.

"Have you seen a gynecologist, Sage?" Emmy asked.

Caroline rolled her eyes. Like Mama, she doesn't enjoy personal conversations.

"I have," I said to Emmy, deadpan.

She can drive me crazy with her creamy "Tell me everything" voice slipping into my bloodstream.

"I saw one in St. Louis on June twenty-sixth for cervical cancer."

"I mean really," Emmy said.

"Yes, really," I replied.

But the truth is, I haven't seen a gynecologist and I don't intend to.

I met Steven Carney at the Farmers Restaurant, where I spent the summer as a hostess, which required that I stand at the front of the restaurant and say, "Welcome to the Farmers."

Steven Carney came in with three women who looked to be in their twenties, and asked for a table for seven.

"I'll have to wait for your whole party to arrive before I seat you, sir," I said.

He told me his whole party was there already and he wanted a table large enough for seven, even though there were only four of them; he would be happy to pay extra for the other three dinners at the rate, say, of pasta primavera at $15.95 without wine or an appetizer.

I seated him at a table for six and took away the extra two chairs to avoid trouble with the manager.

"Your waiter will be Ron." I passed out menus.

Steven Carney grabbed my wrist before I could leave. "Look here," he said.

I put my head close to his in order to hear what he was saying, and what he said was, "Are you black or white?"

No one had ever asked me that.

"White," I said, without missing a beat.

But it is not exactly true.

When he left that night, he gave me an envelope from the Roosevelt Hotel in New York City in which there was a note.

"Thank you for your special consideration. Yours, Steven Carney."

He had enclosed a chocolate kiss.

The following day, there was another note from him, taped to the front door of the rooming house where I was living.

"I got your address from Ron, the waiter. Please meet me for coffee at the Linden at nine a.m." Signed "Steven C."

I didn't go.

That night, he came to the restaurant for dinner again, with a young woman in a lavender sundress and spiked lemon-yellow hair, and asked for a table for four.

"I can't seat you until your entire party has arrived, sir."

"I'm familiar with these rules," he said.

"Very well." I showed him to a table for three and took out one of the chairs.

"Your waitress this evening will be Beth." I handed a menu to his friend and then one to him.

He grabbed my wrist. "Can you tell me where the men's is?" he asked.

I pointed and he got up.

But he didn't go to the men's room. He followed me to the front of the restaurant, where I had resumed my post as hostess, took my hand, and asked me if I would come to his place that night.

"No," I said.

I wasn't graceful. No one had ever asked me to his place before and I didn't know how to respond. But I did look at his dark curly head, at the size of his broad hands, with what I now recognize as desire.

"Then I'll come to yours," he said nonchalantly.

"I'll probably be out," I replied, and later I told the manager I felt suddenly ill.

At the public phone on the street, I called Emmy, who lives with her husband and baby daughter in Boston. I said I had to come to Boston because of an awful time I was having with my boyfriend.

"Of course. We'll meet you at the ferry," Emmy said, but she was tentative. "I'm surprised you have a boyfriend and have never mentioned him to us."

"Well, I do," I said, "and he's driving me crazy."

I have never had a boyfriend, although I dream about love affairs all the time. Romance is compli-

cated in my family, and as the youngest, I have seen
trouble and I'm careful. Emmy had an abortion the
day before her twentieth birthday, and Caroline,
unsuited to commitment, has had a "reputation"
since I can remember. What Mama knew of romance with our father broke her heart. I have
crushes and in a single evening can invent a relationship from its inception through a torrent of
kisses and tears. I have a framed picture on my wall
in this dorm room of an unbearably handsome boy
from high school named Buck O'Hanolan, but the
"Love forever and ever, Buck" was written to my
oldest friend, Jessica, not me, and Jessica gave me
the picture when they broke up. I'm careful by nature, sensing in myself a capacity for passion out of
control.

I missed the last ferry to Woods Hole, and called
Emmy to say I had changed my mind. As it turned
out, Steven Carney never came to the rooming
house where I was staying.

My father is black and I've never seen him. He left
before I was born, after asking my mother, who was
at the time three months pregnant with me, would
she get an abortion, which she refused to do. This

news I learned not from my mother, but from my aunt Winona, in the interest of full disclosure. It's an example of why certain character types should avoid the helping professions.

The story of my father that my family has chosen to tell was told to me by my mother and by Emmy, who remembers him with a kind of thrill.

In the summer after her freshman year at the University of Wisconsin, my mother went to Mississippi to help the effort of civil rights workers in turning out the vote. She was young and wildly excited about living away from the middle-class neighborhood where her own parents had struggled financially to bring up children who would contribute to the continuation of society as they knew it. Not the society my mother hoped to inherit. She went to Mississippi with her boyfriend, Harry Broome, who was bent on saving the world, and was with Harry when she met John Taylor, who is my father.

She simply fell in love with him, Emmy tells me.

"Simply" is probably the wrong word, because their love affair outraged my grandparents in St. Louis, outraged my grandparents in Mississippi, now dead, and also Harry Broome, who tried to kill my father with an L. L. Bean knife and ended up cooling off in jail.

So, as anyone can see, the romantic stakes were very high and lasted at a certain pitch through the births of one after the other of us—Emmy, Jacob, then Caroline, when my parents were still living in Mississippi. They left when my father was asked to serve on the Civil Rights Commission in Washington, D.C., and my mother was pregnant with Tobias.

Things fell apart quickly in Washington. The fire was out for my father by the time Tobias was born—this from Emmy, who suggested that I never mention it to Mama, who prefers to think that my father's political ambition made an interracial marriage impossible.

Emmy told me the decision was not entirely his.

My mother had said that if he left her, even for a day or a weekend, he would never be allowed back. He could have no contact with his children except through letters, which he did write regularly and for a long time. To Emmy and Jacob and Caroline and Tobias. Sometimes he added, "And the baby." Although Emmy, who wrote to him, had told him my name was Lilly Sage Taylor, called Lilly for my grandmother in St. Louis.

We are all called Sage. It was my father's favorite name, and since my mother chose our Christian names from her own midwestern white Methodist family, my father had the choice of our middle names and he chose Sage. Emily Sage, Jacob Sage, Caroline Sage, Tobias Sage, and me, Lilly Sage, called Sage instead of Lilly at my own insistence since I turned twelve.

All this happened years ago, and gradually a

sense of our father slipped away from our lives, filled up by Mama—Dr. Louisa Taylor, professor of pediatrics.

What Mama did when he left her in Washington was "remarkable," Aunt Winona says. Mama was thirty-two years old, with four children and another on the way. She packed the clothes, gave all the furniture in the rented house on T and 20th to the Salvation Army, and in mid-December drove a VW van without a working heater to St. Louis. She moved into a rowhouse next door to Aunt Winona, enrolled at Washington University as an undergraduate and then went to medical school, where she specialized in pediatric cardiology. I don't remember an evening in all of those years when we didn't sit down at the dining room table to a hot dinner with candles, whether Mama was on duty at the hospital or at home.

My father wasn't a subject of conversation at the dinner table, but we talked about him whenever our mother was not around. We talked about their marriage with a sense of romance, as if we were the products of a rare, sweet union destroyed by the circuitous progress of history.

My family has stories that get repeated, and according to Jacob, the stories tend in the reporting to be more true in substance than they are in fact.

My favorite is a story about our father, the only one in a large canon of family mythology that is critical of our mother, and we tell it behind her back. In this story, our father, struggling financially as a principled black man in the late civil rights movement, is slowly crowded out of his tiny house on T Street in Washington, D.C., with one after another white baby. Finally, in despair, overpowered by this sainted dynamo of a woman, he leaves before the arrival of his one true heir.

The children in my family look more like my mother, who is tall and slender and very fair, of Scandinavian and Irish descent. Except me. So my father couldn't lay claim as kin by appearance to any one of us but me. And me, he's never seen.

When Steven Carney said he wanted to know whether I was black or white, I should have told him the truth, because I am my father's daughter, even though I have never seen him. But I think about him and what it might have been like to have a father, to know him, to call him on the telephone and ask him to come after Steven Carney, who is at this very moment trying to push open the door to my bedroom on the fourth floor of Emerson Hall.

Chapter Two

If Steven Carney comes in here—and he's making that breathing sound right now—*whoo, whoo, whoo,* like sex under the door. I suppose it's like sex—but how would I know, you ask me, and of course you're right. If he does come in, if he manages to break down the door to do whatever he has in mind to do, I ought to be dressed, not lying naked on top of my comforter.

So I slip off the bed and put on my black trousers, the only ones that fit since I started to expand

three weeks ago, and a T-shirt from Tobias with
"Me Too" written in red, whatever that means.

It's almost six and the sky is turning the silver-
gray of autumn dawn, a damp cool gray that I like
because a gray day doesn't make demands.

Soon I'll be able to call my mother. She sets her
alarm for six, then turns it off and resets it for seven
so she'll be half awake by the second time it rings. I
could call her now. If I called now, she would think
it was the hospital—unlike ordinary mothers who
aren't doctors, she doesn't think a call in the early
morning is the announcement of personal disaster.

I'm concerned about the bathroom. I have a sink
in my bedroom and there's a bathroom down the
hall, yet since I became aware that Steven Carney is
following me, I haven't left my room.

I had just finished organic chemistry lab—I forget
whether that was yesterday, or days ago, time has a
way of slipping—and I saw Steven Carney, on the
corner in front of the library, catch sight of me
walking out of the science building. He was across
the street but I watched him take me into account.
You can always tell that sort of thing.

He crossed to my side of the street, and I
watched him coming toward me in a hurry. I
should have said "Yes?" in a challenging voice.
"Anything I can do for you?" But I didn't.

My heart leapt into my mouth and I headed straight to my dorm, out of breath. I wasn't even running. I couldn't possibly have run with my lungs collapsing the way they were. As I fumbled for the key, I could see him behind me in the smoky glass of the door. He was so close he might have said "Sage" in a friendly way, though if he did, I didn't hear him.

I headed up the steps to the fourth floor, not waiting for the elevator, my backpack weighted with books, chemistry and invertebrate biology, so heavy I thought I'd have to leave them at the first landing.

A boy named Dave, with fluffy red hair and a lisp, and the kind of ease I'd die for, was standing near my room as I fled down the corridor.

"Hiya, speedo," he said.

I'm sure he was trying to be friendly, but I didn't have the presence of mind to respond. I rushed by him into my room and locked the door.

I heard Steven Carney ask Dave whether he knew a girl named Sage and Dave said, "Yes," and Steve asked where I lived and, without much enthusiasm, Dave said, "There," and "There," of course, is here.

So Steven came to my door in daylight and banged on it, and the *whoo, whoo, whoo*ing under the door started after dark.

I'm not surprised Steven Carney has come after me. You know when a person is getting fixed on you. Steven's interest is what Aunt Winona delicately refers to as "carnal." Although I'm inexperienced with carnal matters, so you make your own judgments about my reliability—I swear it has to do with race.

He wants to find out who I am inside my taffy skin, and does my blood run black as night. That's news I'd like to learn myself, not with the assistance of Steven Carney.

At the moment, the bathroom, and what to do about it, is a serious logistical problem. When I arrived at this dormitory and asked where was the ladies' room on my floor and went into a cubicle and locked the door and sat down and happened to look at the feet in the cubicle next to mine, to see that they belonged to a man, also sitting down, because the feet were pointing out, I almost died.

Since then, the bathroom has been in the way of my adjusting to university life. So far I've taken only four showers, and those by setting my alarm for three in the morning, thinking, correctly, that very few people will be interested in showers at that hour.

The problem with the bathroom has existed before, but now it is by way of an emergency.

I believe he is calling my name. Certainly "Sage" is what he whispers under the door, his voice sailing

up like scent to the bed where I was lying, now
sitting, my arms around my knees, my heart flip-
flopping in my mouth like the goldfish I held
against my tongue until it died—a part of initiation
into high school, a place I hated as much as I hate
this university. Then at least I spent the nights in
my own bed.

Outside my window, dawn has the silver glisten
of morning. There is the welcome scuttle of a new
day in a small city, noisy with the clatter of delivery
trucks pulling up to the restaurants along the street
where I live, the slam of metal as their rear doors
slide open, the hearty shouts of workers.

Perhaps Steven Carney thinks I've left this room,
slipped out the window, dropped to the street on
sheets tied together or a rope, or jumped the four
floors to the little patch of grass beneath my window, or climbed down a giant oak wild with acorns
promising a long winter.

I could jump. I am athletic. At least I was in high
school in St. Louis, before I started to expand.

I was raised white in a white neighborhood, with
almost no black people for blocks around, no blacks
in my section of high school, nobody thinking me
anything but lily-white Irish, probably Catholic.
Who cared what I looked like in my neighborhood?
I was what I seemed to be, and that was white.

No one gave consideration to my race except Mazie Drew, who's the color of bark and has her own crowd. I like her and she likes me. We used to go to Ernie's Sub Shop after soccer and smoke. She'd look at me from under those lidded eyes of hers, her bluesy voice low in her throat, and tell me I was a make-believe white woman squandering my chances at a real life.

We didn't keep it a secret we were half black. But we didn't make an issue of it either.

I pass. A milk-chocolate girl with frizzy dark hair, not black, not nappy, really, but Brillo-pad frizzy. And gray eyes with big black pupils, almost the size of the iris.

"*Born startled,*" Mama told me once.

Frightened is closer to the truth.

From the time I can remember the early things, like the blue wild flowers papering the wall beside my crib, or the taste of honey-vanilla ice cream on my tongue, or the smell of gasoline in the shed out back, I have felt uneasy in the world.

"Sage is extrasensitive," is what Mama says about me.

"Brain-tweaked," Tobias says, with his gift for the visual. "All the electrical wires sticking out of her head sizzling away like cooked hamburger."

I've kept a Fear List since I was six years old. Sometimes I put it in my underwear drawer, sometimes under my mattress, checking it over, crossing and adding, one year to the next, one month to the next. Yet no matter how many fears I cross out—poison toadstools and copperheads and Tylenol with cyanide from Osco Drug—the list gets longer every time I look at it.

At school, I keep the list in my *Webster's Collegiate* between pages 486 and 487, "fatigue" to "feature," where "fear" is listed—*Fear, a distressing emotion aroused by impending danger, evil, or pain, whether the threat is real or imagined; the feeling or condition of being afraid.*

That is my permanent condition. I don't remember a time in my life without it, which may be why Steven Carney is lurking outside my door like an attack dog, sniffing fear on me, the perfume of sex.

I have this crazy sense of order you'd never imagine if you met me—this way of always doing something in the same sequence, of cleaning out the corners of rooms, of eating one thing at a time—all the meat, all the vegetables, et cetera—of dressing from bottom to top, socks, shoes, underpants, pants, bra, shirt, sweater, teeth, face, hair.

I don't want to misrepresent myself. I'm not one of these overeducated compulsive middle-class white girls spilling out of the bathrooms of universities, where they've been washing the skin off their hands or throwing up the meal they just ate. If you met me, you'd think: Funny, Sweet, Good-Natured, Nothing Special. Just nice.

Lilly Sage Taylor. Age: Eighteen. Height: Five-two. Weight: Fat. Race: Whatever. Don't bother to ask personal questions. This is the nineties in the United States of America, and you are expected to line up single file with your own kind. If you happen to know what kind that is. And who does?

I seem ordinary, an outwardly cheerful young woman, spreading amoeba-like without a nucleus, in different shapes depending on the environment, always the same mass and density but in varying configurations. That's how I seem. It's not how I am, of course. If I were, I'd be Miss Congeniality, brain-dead on the subject of fear.

My present Fear List has two hundred forty-seven items—eighty-six have been crossed out since I started keeping the list, but I hold on to the same list I've had since I was small so I'll have a sense of progress.

It's comforting to sit on a bed as I'm doing now—even with Steven Carney deep-breathing on the other side of my door—and read my list. Like photographs, it gives me a sense of a history, of belonging to the world, in this place, at this time. Of continuing.

Disappearing is the real fear. Sometimes I'm afraid that for no apparent reason, I will suddenly cease to exist.

I don't know whether that fear is a wish or a terror. I feel as if I were going to melt down, fade into nothing, run like watercolors across a sheet of paper. And what will be left of me then? Certainly no presence of human shape. An aura, perhaps, ash after a fire, a chemical residue. But for me, whatever that is, a disappearing consciousness of self, there will be only fear, distilled to its purest form.

There are ten items, running a third of the way down the last page of my present Fear List.

1. Salmon (Matthew Hooker died April 12 this year in Barnes Hospital of poisoned salmon. I read the obits.)
2. Ebola virus (I read everything medical. I even buy *Science* magazine at the newsstand for virus updates.)
3. Breast cancer (One out of seven women will get it.)
4. Gynecologists (Personal reasons for fear. No stats on death by gynecologists.)
5. Throat closing from enlarged epiglottis

6. Airplanes
7. *Legionella* from air-conditioning (I read that a lot of people died in a Philadelphia hotel some time ago. That made an impression on me.)
8. Hotels (Because of *Legionella* and fires. Motels okay.)
9. Sex
10. Steven Carney

Sex is on every page since seventh grade. I thought about sex before then, but in the abstract. I didn't use to feel in danger.

I've been looking for my father in an orderly way since we cleaned out the attic of our rowhouse in St. Louis and divided his things among the five of us. We each got pictures and letters, some to my mother when they were still together, some to us.

His name is John Jefferson Taylor, and though John Taylor is a common name—there are about twenty of them in the Jackson, Mississippi, telephone book alone—John Jefferson Taylor is not.

What I did, beginning in February of my senior year in high school, was to organize a private search through the telephone directories of major cities from St. Louis east and north and south. I haven't told anyone. I don't even know whether anyone in my family wants him found except Jacob.

Most days since then, I've called about ten John Taylors. I started in St. Louis and have just finished Chicago.

"Is John Jefferson Taylor there?" I ask when someone picks up the phone. I figure that way a person will say either no or yes. And I won't have to explain or stay on the phone too long by tracking down every John Taylor listed in the books.

So far there have been two John Jefferson Taylors. The one in New Orleans was certainly white, northern, and probably drunk. He thought I was Maxine, a woman he didn't seem to like.

The other John Jefferson Taylor was in Jackson. For the first few minutes of the conversation I knew this was it, and my heart was beating so fast I thought I would die. His voice was low and southern and a little bored.

"Yes," he said. He was John Jefferson Taylor, fifty-two years old and divorced. Yes, he had five children he knew of, maybe more. No, he hadn't seen them for a long time because his wife, whom he referred to as "the bitch," wouldn't let him.

"Is your wife white?" I asked.

"White?" John Jefferson Taylor asked, his voice falling cotton-soft from his tongue. "Is my wife white, did you say?"

"That's what I was wondering."

"Now what would I have done a thing like that for, sweetheart?" he asked.

"I don't know." I was embarrassed. "I just wondered."

"Next time"—he laughed almost joyously—"next time, now you mention it, she'll be milk-white with a little red pussy."

I hung up then. I was in over my head.

I have only one good picture of my father. Most of mine are blurry, taken with an old Brownie camera, and the color is washed out. But the one I love was probably taken in Mississippi during the Movement, probably by my mother. I can tell it's one she loved too—the way he's standing in rolled-up jeans and a T-shirt, one bare foot on a tree stump, looking straight at the camera. "Sardonic" might be the word to describe his smile, a little grin, one eyebrow higher than the other, his right thumb tucked into his jeans, his fingers long. I bet it's just the way she wanted to think of him when they fell in love. It's the way I've chosen to know him. I have the picture on the table beside my bed.

The telephone is ringing and the alarm clock on my desk says seven-thirty. I must have fallen asleep some time ago. I don't answer the phone. It could be the dean. She's called three times this week. It could be my organic chemistry professor. I let the answering machine pick up.

"Lilly Sage Taylor," the voice says. "You bum. You never call."

It's Jessica Conger. Jess is my best friend since first grade, and she calls me from London, where she's studying the harpsichord. I talked to her in September.

"It's Wednesday," she says, "and I really need to talk to you on the double. What's the matter? Have you died? Dried up? Disappeared?"

I put my hands over my ears and wait for her to hang up.

I wouldn't want you to misunderstand. I love Jess. I simply don't want to talk to her on the telephone.

I do call my family at least once every day, but it's too late now to call my mother. She's already gone to the hospital. I wait for Jess to hang up and dial Jacob. He's probably at the hospital too, so I dial his apartment and leave a message on his machine. I never talk to him except by answering machine, but that's okay. He's interested primarily in my academics because I'm premed, and I give him that news on the machine. Emmy is interested in my life, particularly the incidentals of my sexual activity, which I invent for her.

"Hi, Jacob," I say to his machine. "It's Wednesday, and I just got back from running and I'm on my way to chem class where I got an A on the last test. I hope surgery rotation is okay and there's not too much free-floating blood. Talk to you tomorrow."

Mostly Jacob sends me postcards—sweet ones, about three times a week, so my mailbox will be full. He must have gone to the drugstore near the hospital and picked up about fifty of the same picture of the St. Louis Arch.

"Dear Sage," he'll write in his scrawly about-to-be-a-doctor hand. "Moving to gastroenterology tomorrow. Wiped out from late nights. Miss you lots and lots. Hugs, Jacob."

That sort of note. But he doesn't call. He's not good on the telephone unless he has a subject like blood sugar to discuss. He's always been that way.

I try Caroline, and she answers on the first ring.

"Hiya," I say.

"Jeez, Sage. It's the crack of dawn. Don't you ever sleep?"

"I've got a nine-o'clock and I've got to go running first. Are you okay?" I say.

"Swell."

I hear her stretching and yawning. "Wanna talk to Faustie?" she asks.

Faustie is her yellow cat and I don't really want to talk to him, but Caroline insists.

Caroline has the studied look of an artist, always slightly abstracted and unfocused, askew, as if the left and the right don't exactly match up. She dresses messy-funk; her hands, even her face, are patched with paint; and she has a way of looking at things, an amazed cocaine look, although I don't think she does cocaine. Her style of conversation—she learned it in art school—is New York quippy and impenetrable. But I know Caroline very well inside, and she's pudding like me, with a more refined defense system.

"So how far have you been running lately?" She always asks about my running. Caroline does not do sports. Painting and sex are the full measure of her athletic activity.

"Five miles," I say.

"Not every day. You shouldn't. That's too much."

"No, but I'll run this morning," I say.

"How's what's-his-name?"

"Saint Paul?"

Saint Paul is a sophomore here whom I told her I go out with, because that story pleases her; it makes her think I'm normal. There is a Paul in my chemistry lab, but I've never spoken to him. He's white, with terrible acne and beige mousy hair. I have no plans to strike up a friendship.

"Has anything happened between you?" This is surprising for Caroline, who almost never takes a personal interest, except occasionally in sex.

"Not everything," I say. "I mean, you know."

"I know."

She certainly does know. Caroline has been doing everything since she was thirteen.

"Just kissing and stuff," I say.

"But he doesn't spend the night?"

"Not yet," I say. "I want to be sure."

"Smart, Sagie," she tells me.

I ask about Tobias, who's left his coaching job, and then I hang up.

I tell my family what they want to hear. Not the truth. The truth would kill them after the year we've had.

I'm listening for Steven Carney when the telephone rings. I have it on six rings before the machine picks up; this time, it's the dean. I haven't met her, but she has called before.

"This is Dean Showel calling Sage Taylor," she says. "Sage. I'd like for you to call my office. I have notes from your chemistry professor and your invertebrate biology professor that you have missed the last three weeks of class.''

I turn down the machine so I don't have to listen to the dean. And I don't want Steven Carney to hear her either.

Chapter Three

Emmy was asleep when Sage called at eight forty-five, on a gloomy, sunless morning in Boston. Maggie, her daughter, was sleeping too, sucking her tiny fingers.

"Did I wake you?" Sage asked, cheerful, always cheerful. "You sound wiped out."

"I sort of am," Emmy said.

"I always wait till after I figure Jack's gone to work to call you, so you can get organized," Sage said.

"He's gone to work." Emmy sat up. "It's just that Maggie kept waking in the night and I'm exhausted. Are you okay?" Her sister's voice sounded thin.

"I'm fine," Sage said. "I have a calculus quiz in ten minutes, so I was just checking in."

It was crazy the way they asked each other that—grown children of a pediatrician, with a social worker aunt. "Are you okay?" they'd say to one another and then, lying easily, "Of course, I'm just fine. I'm A-okay."

"Well, call me later," Emmy said. "I'll be here mostly."

Emmy got up and wandered through the living room, into the kitchen, holding Maggie over her shoulder. The new puppy had peed by the sink and now lay under the table, happily chewing on Maggie's stuffed mouse. Emmy sat down at the kitchen table and regarded the puddle of urine with mild indifference.

"No, no," she said softly, but she didn't take the mouse from the puppy's small mouth.

When the telephone in the kitchen rang a second time, Emmy made no effort to pick it up, listening instead to the message being left at high volume.

"Em, it's Jacob." Her brother's deep voice filled the room. "I have surgery this morning until ten or so, but I want to talk to you sometime today about the house. Winona thinks we should sell it."

Emmy crossed her legs under herself and rested Maggie in the cradle of her lap.

She wasn't ready to talk to Jacob about the house. Or Winona. She wasn't ready to talk to Winona about anything. Maybe Jacob had called Caroline. She dialed her sister's number in Philadelphia. She liked talking to Caroline, efficient, like Mama, unflappable, or so she seemed.

Tobias answered the telephone at Caroline's.

"Hi," Emmy said. "It's your big sister."

"I know," Tobias said. "Of course I know who it is."

He sounded drunk. He wouldn't be drunk before nine in the morning, but he was probably stoned. It made Emmy angry to hear his gravy-thick voice, and so she said, straight off, exactly what she should not have said.

"How come you quit your job?"

"I was fired," Tobias said.

"How can you be fired from a coaching job?" Emmy's voice was flying up the register. "No one gets fired from a high school coaching job."

"I was late too often, so I was fired. Pretty simple."

"And now you'll have time to get a lot of rest,"

Emmy said crossly. "Sleep in, sleep all day, get to bed early."

"Right," Tobias said without rancor.

"I'm calling to find out if Jacob or Sage called this morning."

"Not Jacob," Tobias said. "But Sage did yesterday. You can count on Sage calling every day."

"Did she seem okay?"

"Dunno. I didn't talk to her."

"I have this intuition."

Emmy lived on intuitions—getting by, vision to vision, without a capacity for much order, little common sense but complete faith in her own instincts.

"Keep your intuitions private, Em. You have too many of them," Tobias said. "Here's Caroline. Tell her."

"I'm worried about Sage," Emmy said when Caroline got on the phone.

"Don't be," Caroline answered. "She sounded great when I last talked to her. How come you're worried?"

"I just am. I worry about everything lately."

"Don't worry about Sage. She's always cheerful."

"I know. She is with me too. I don't understand how she can be."

"People are amazing when they have to be," Caroline said. "I'm sure Sage is okay."

"Maybe she is," Emmy said. "Did Jacob call you about the house?"

"He wouldn't dare. He knows I refuse to sell it."

"So do I. Even though I can't imagine living in St. Louis again."

"If we say no, maybe Jacob will finally give up trying," Caroline said.

"I hope so. That's what I said the last time I talked to him."

"And don't worry about Sage," Caroline said. "Feed Maggie and clean your apartment, and call me later."

Emmy laughed and said okay and good-bye.

The apartment was a mess. That morning before he left for work, in a rare outburst, Jack had said the place was a pigsty. He couldn't stand to come home to it at night.

"I can't help it," Emmy had answered. She knew Jack was right. But some days she couldn't do a thing for thinking about Mama.

In fact, Maggie made her think about Mama particularly now that she was the mother of a first daughter herself. Her parents had been no more than children in a war zone in Mississippi when Emmy was born. She found herself looking at her hands, at her profile as she passed her bedroom mirror—hands like her mother's, a profile like her mother's, her hair frizzy but red like Mama's had been when she was young. It was Caroline who acted like her mother, but Emmy was her mother in appearance.

She put Maggie in her carriage and slid onto the couch with a brightly illustrated food magazine. Later she'd do the dishes, sweep the kitchen floor, take the vacuum cleaner out of the closet.

Chapter Four

There's a pattern to my day here so I don't go crazy, trapped as I now am by Steven Carney. I have a shoe box full of pictures of my parents and my father's letters to my mother, which I brought from the house in St. Louis. I'm putting them in order so that the history of my family will open to include me.

I spend hours in this tiny airless dormitory room, reading over letters, staring at photographs, until a conversation that might have been in progress as the camera clicked comes to life in my mind.

My childhood seemed ordinary, but it wasn't. The simple reality of growing up white with a black father—absent because he wasn't allowed to be present, or so I've been told—in a family in which I am the only child who looks black—or perhaps it is better to say the only child who does not, on careful examination, look white—has created some difficulties for me.

On this October morning, sunny with a little wind, the smell of winter in the trees, the difficulties seem insurmountable.

When I was in junior high school, we were asked to write an essay on race for a statewide competition. According to our teacher, Miss Purchase, the seventh-grade class at North County Junior High had, through no fault of its own, inherited responsibility for the Missouri Compromise, which had allowed Missouri to be admitted to the Union in 1821 as a slave state and Maine as a free state in order to preserve the balance of free and slave states. Race has always been a sensitive issue in the history of Missouri, and especially in St. Louis.

"What is race?" was the question—five hundred words, double-spaced.

School has always been easy for me. I go without much anxiety, and until recently wouldn't have considered missing a class. But on the afternoon when this assignment was given out, when Miss Purchase whispered, "What is race?" across the grid of desks, five deep, five across, dreary seventh-graders waiting for the bell, I became instantly sick.

I stayed home for two weeks with an undiagnosed illness; my own conclusion was early lupus, whose description I found in my mother's medical dictionary.

My mother wrote a note to Miss Purchase saying I wouldn't be participating in the statewide competition, and Miss Purchase called to say every child at North County was participating. She gave my mother a lesson on the Missouri Compromise and added that a Taylor child, above all children in North County, should be included in a contest about race.

"Sage declines," my mother answered coolly.

I know the history of my family well enough to make up stories true in spirit, if not in fact. That is why I am spending hours in this room looking at the same picture until it is imprinted intaglio on my mind.

By arranging the photographs in the order that they were written, by imagining with each one a story for the moment captured by the camera, I hope to understand how I came to be in this place. By which I mean this mental and emotional place— not the tiny airless dormitory room from which I'm writing.

ME and John Jefferson, August, 1964

*T*his Mama has written on the back of the earliest picture I have of them.

The scene is a clapboard house with a weeping back porch and a small scraggly tree against which my father leans. My mother is in a long skirt, naked from the waist up, her arms folded across her breasts, her posture combative. John Jefferson, my father, wears jeans and a dress shirt with the collar open and the sleeves rolled up.

"So what are you doing coming here to see me without your shirt on, Louisa?"

She throws her head back and glares at him. "My shirt was stolen when I was going door to door on Ash Street registering the vote. That's why I'm here."

"Who took your shirt?" John Jefferson asks.

"The Jackson city police," she says.

He reaches out to touch her bare arm.

"I'm sorry for that, Louisa. I'm sorry that had to happen to you." He takes her hand. "You come on in here."

She follows him up the broken back steps, through a ratty screen door into the kitchen, where coffee is brewing and the smell of bacon lingers in the corners of the hot room.

He unbuttons his shirt and takes it off, puts it over her shoulders.

"So tell me, what happened?" he asks.

She slips into his shirt and buttons it up to just below her clavicle.

"I was on Ash, at the third house I'd been to this morning, and a policeman walking by shouted at me to stop soliciting, it was against the law. So I said, 'I'm not soliciting,' and he called me a nigger-lover and I didn't say anything back, but the woman who had answered the door told me to 'git,' and shut the door, and then there were three policemen, and the one who had talked to me in the first place took out a little knife and sliced my shirt from top to bottom, and another one held me, and another one pulled it off and pinched my nipple hard between his fingers, and they all laughed."

"You should go back to St. Louis, Louisa," John says, *and he's leaning over her, taking her hands into his, kissing her fingers.*

"I might have gone back to St. Louis before I met you," she says, *"but I can't very well go back now."*

"I'll go with you," he says.

"I don't think we'll be very welcome at my family's house." She laughs. *"My parents, as you might imagine, had their hearts set on Harry Broome."*

"So?" he says, *putting his hands under her arms, pulling her against his bare chest, kissing her full lips.*

We all were given letters. We didn't get to read them first and then choose which ones we wanted to keep. That would have taken weeks, and we didn't have weeks. So Jacob divided them, ten each, paying attention to the dates so we'd each have a spread of our parents' lives. Certain ones I read over more than others; in them, there seems to be a man, a story about a man, not just information as in the other letters I ended up with. They are written in bright blue ink, as if color was a signature with

him, and difficult to decipher, the handwriting large
and slanted, headed downhill.

May 26, 1964

Louisa baby, I've gone home to Sunflower, without having a chance to let you know although I
asked Bosco to tell you my Mama has taken sick
unto death and I had to go in a hurry.

I don't know what to think or what to do
about our confetti baby growing like trouble in
your belly, except to come back to Jackson and
marry you—you and me hanging off a kite high
above the city, flying west to a perfect conclusion.

You're the love of my life.

JJT

September 1, 1964

Dear Louisa, God, we're young. I thought about
that this morning when I woke up in the bed I
was born in, and thought you're nineteen and I'm
twenty and we don't know what it's going to
mean, us two together with a baby. Sure as hell
we can't live in Mississippi. Or St. Louis. I hear
okay things about Chicago.

John

P.S. I met the sister of one of the civil rights
workers who were killed near Philadelphia. Mi-
chael Schwerner. She was at church with my

cousin Everett, who's a preacher here. The sister's tall and skinny and wears her hair up in one of those floppy buns to make her seem old. But she is so young. I couldn't stop looking at her.

On the bottom of a card from my father, there's a note in Mama's handwriting: "John gave me a silver mirror to go with this card. He got it at an antique store in Jackson, and the initials, even though it was engraved for someone else, are the same as mine. LST. Such a funny, odd present, but sweet."

To Louisa Taylor, the card with the initialed mirror says. *On our wedding day, October 4, 1964. So you can see what beauty I see whenever I look at you. From your loving husband, John Jefferson Taylor.*

The Taylor Family, September, 1967,
at 111 Olive Street, Jackson, Mississippi,
the day after the Klan threw a makeshift bomb
at our house in the middle of the night

The house looks spruced up, white with green
shutters, yellow flowers in a big pot on the front
porch. But not entirely spruced up. To the left of
the porch, the burned-out remains of what must
have been a wing to the first floor hang off the main
house in black charred pieces like parts of a jigsaw
puzzle.

Mama is sitting on the top step of the porch
holding Jacob. John Taylor leans against the railing
with Emmy, maybe three years old, on his shoul-

ders, and beside them a mangy brown dog with a head too big for its body stares stupidly into the camera.

"I'm getting to be afraid, John," Louisa says, her voice softer than normal, none of the familiar sass the people who know her are used to.

"There's reason," John says, shifting Emmy on his shoulders. *"I don't know what we should do, but I can't leave Mississippi. Not now. Maybe you and the children should go home for a while, or to my papa's."*

"To St. Louis?" Louisa asks. *"I don't think so."*

"You can go home without any trouble," John says. *"These children look as white as you do."*

"That's not what I mean. I don't have any interest in going back to Missouri. I have an interest in both of us leaving Mississippi." She puts her head against his legs and closes her eyes.

"Soon," he says. *"Soon we can move, maybe to Washington, but not now."* He takes hold of her long red braid and pulls it. *"Where's your fire, sweetheart? You used to love the heat."*

Louisa shrugs. *"Before the children,"* she says. *"I liked a lot of things, like trouble, before the children were born."*

"Like me?" John asks, lowering his eyes at her.

"Shut up, John Jefferson Taylor." Louisa laughs and walks over to the burned-out wing of the house.

She shakes her head. "We were lucky," she says. "We could have gone up in flames."

"They won't be back to bother us," he says. "I promise you that. They've got a short attention span."

September 24, 1967

So baby, things got a little unpleasant after you left and now we've got a problem. I've enclosed the article from the Jackson paper about the house and the story Bill Garlin wrote about us—he's that nice man who goes all-out, but he had a cross-burning in his front yard last Thursday, so he won't be going all-out for long.

I hope things are okay in St. Louis, that your Ma is not too busy checking our babies for black genes and your Pa is getting better after his heart attack. Tell him from me that it's not good for a man's heart to hate so bad he can taste it.

I don't know what we're going to do about the house. There's a lot of smoke damage and it smells bad—and as you can see, the front door got blown off. Bosco offered to let us live with him, which is okay. But not perfect.

JJT

P.S. I feel terrible about Marco, dumb dog sleeping on the couch like he's a human being.

It looks like we may just get out of the Olive Street lease without having to pay for attracting the attention of the Klan—in which case we can just rent another house, a small place, one suited to a man of my color and station. Tell your parents that.

A newspaper photograph shows the house with a large rectangle blown out in the center. You can see the living room, the fireplace, a couch, a rug, a bookcase, and a child's climbing gym. There's no front door or bay window, what's left of the porch collected in a wood pile along the front. The article reads:

FREEDOM WORKERS' HOUSE BURNED BY KLAN

John and Louisa Taylor, freedom workers in Jackson since 1963, who live at 111 Olive Street, lost part of their house last night when a bomb was thrown through the front window into the living room, destroying the front of the house. John Jefferson Taylor, age 23, a black man from Sunflower, was in the house at the time and escaped through the back window. Mrs. Taylor, who is white, and the couple's two children were out of town visiting her family in Missouri. A family dog was injured in the blast and had to be put down. The Ku Klux Klan is under suspicion, although no action has been taken.

November 1, for chrissake

Darling, this trip of yours is going on too long for me, but I have good news. I rented a house with four bedrooms and a nice fenced backyard—$150 a month plus utilities—and I move there tomorrow. Come home. It's deathlonely here without you and Emmy and Jacob.

JJT

Me, John, Emmy, and Jacob at our new house
on Congress Street, Jackson, Mississippi,
Thanksgiving, 1967

This is my favorite picture—maybe my favorite of all of the pictures I have of my mother. There's Mama first, in jeans and a turtleneck, her hair falling over her shoulders. Just by the look of her, I can tell she felt beautiful. And happy. I've never seen another picture of my mother purely happy, without an edge of something—worry or temper or determination—but this picture hasn't got an edge of anything but happiness. Emmy is next to her, hands in the pockets of her overalls, hair sticking straight up in a thin pole of a ponytail, and then there's John Taylor, holding Jacob, who looks to be crying. What I like about John Taylor in this picture is that he's peering over at Mama, as if he can't take his eyes off her, as if he could eat her up.

Chapter Five

In my first week at this university, I began to have trouble breathing.

It happened while I was dressing for an eight-o'clock chemistry lab that met in the science building across campus. Already late, I was standing naked with a small pile of discarded possibilities on the floor around me, when, out of nowhere, I had a breathing attack.

Clothes are not a matter of serious consideration in my life. I simply wear them—long and wide over my rear, extra-large white tees and black pants, dark men's shirts with the sleeves rolled up, and long Indian cotton skirts, clunky shoes, bulky sweaters in olive drab or gray. No color, ever.

I look intentionally normal so as to fade into the human geography. In terms of fashion, I'd be happy in former Communist China, where people wore Mao jackets and square-cut trousers. Or in the military. Uniforms are ideal.

I don't have a look like Caroline does in her striped men's ties holding back her short, stick-out black hair, long purple silk shirts unbuttoned to her breasts, shiny bright red skirts and Doc Martens.

Emmy has a look as well, a black look, tiny black tops with tight long sleeves to show her pencil-thin arms to advantage, black sari pants, even when she was pregnant. She wears her frizzy hair long like I do. But my look, if you want to call it that, is Gap men's wear, with a sports bra flattening the pendulous breasts I'd be happy to exchange for hard labor. I'm androgynous, and that look is an entirely satisfactory disguise.

When I had breathing trouble the first time, I sat down on my bed, struggling for breath, and called Emmy. I don't ordinarily let my family know bad news, but certain that my lungs had collapsed and I was on my way out of the world, I dialed Emmy's number in Boston.

"What's the matter?" Emmy asked when I

choked into the receiver. "Sagie, please. Are you okay?"

"I can't breathe," I answered. "I really can't breathe at all."

"Lie down, then." Her voice was suddenly calm; the familiar still authority of Mama's voice surprising in her.

I was immediately glad I had called.

"Put your hands over your mouth and nose and breathe gently," she said. "Okay?"

"Okay," I said.

"In and out, in and out," she went on coaching. "Sage?"

I couldn't answer. I was lying down as she had told me to, the telephone pressed against my ear so I could listen, breathing in and out of my cupped hands. I made a sound to assure her that I had not stopped breathing altogether.

"I think you may be having a panic attack," Emmy said.

"Maybe," I agreed.

"What were you doing?"

"Nothing. Just getting dressed for chemistry lab."

"Maybe you're worried about chemistry lab?"

"Maybe."

I know about panic attacks. They are Aunt Winona's preferred subject for dinner-table conversation. She is always seeing tendencies, especially in me, wishing panic on us so she can take the role of scientific sleuth and uncover contributing factors.

"A panic attack is a strong and sudden fear," she told us one night this summer, when we were all at home in St. Louis. "I have seen thousands of patients with panic attacks, and I'm very good at discovering the source."

"How can you have seen thousands of patients, Aunt Winona?" Tobias asked. "You must be as old as God."

Winona is not a listener, which must be difficult for the patient who is paying her to listen.

"I don't want to talk about panic attacks, Aunt Winona," Caroline said. "You'll make me have one."

But Aunt Winona sailed forward. "Out of the blue, a perfectly ordinary person is walking happily along and—*panic.*" Her hands, with their long painted fingernails, flew into the air. "Pavlov was right."

Aunt Winona is fond of Pavlov, believing our lives to be governed entirely by conditioned responses and not by genetics. I don't listen to these pronouncements from Aunt Winona. I don't have to. They are repeated so frequently and with such unbridled enthusiasm that osmosis takes over and they slip through my skin into my bloodstream.

Nevertheless, lying on my bed, breathing in and out of my hand, listening to Emmy on the phone, I believed I was having a panic attack.

Later, under my covers, breathing more easily, the phone hung up, I considered the subject of conditioned response.

Breathing trouble, I realized, had been coming on for days. It has occurred to me that attendance at this university, or maybe any university today, requires accommodation, especially on the subjects of race and sex, which I'm not so much unwilling as unable to make.

I'd be happy to live under a system of government uncomplicated by choice, a benign despotic rule, sort of like the condition of childhood, where daily life is governed by certain requirements not of your own choosing. But the mind is your own secret treasure—your imagination can go wild—for who is to say what may climb through the intricate spider webs of your brain?

The first day of orientation, I had to make choices that made no sense for an eighteen-year-old woman immature for her age. One who has been nowhere but downtown St. Louis and Martha's Vineyard, just a girl, really, of a certain height and weight, a certain physical description and IQ, in the process of becoming whoever she's going to be. But no one yet, beyond the genetic promise of intelligence and sensibility and a stubbornness of character.

I had to decide whether I am black or white.

There was information in my mailbox at the university from the African-American House on campus, and an invitation to go there for dinner. They understood I might be interested in their activities. That evening I got a call from one of the sisters.

I was African-American, she said. Wasn't I?

I'm not African. Somebody in the seventeenth century, not named Taylor, but somebody came over from Africa in a slave ship and ended up in Louisiana, and he or she was related to me. That happened almost three hundred years ago. There were Spanish and French people, Creoles and regular old white people who owned slaves in the Delta. Out of that mix of sex and blood came my father, John Jefferson Taylor.

But he is not African and therefore neither am I.

Two women came by my room later that night and asked me personally, face to face—I should have known then the breathing problem would be coming—was I black or white, since I *looked* black.

I have told you that race isn't a subject I seriously considered until this summer when Steven Carney brought it up at the restaurant in Martha's Vineyard.

"I have a black father and a white mother," I told the women.

"That's not what we're talking about," one of them said. She was a real beauty, tall with a high bottom and small breasts and black nappy hair laced with red.

No question, she was black American. Not African, but a mixed-up American like me.

"You'll be no one at this university unless you join," she said. "So you have to decide where your head is. Black or white?"

It was just before supper, but I fell into bed exhausted right after the women left, promising them both that by the next day I'd have made a decision about race.

This is not a decision I can make now.

James Howarth in my seventh-grade class won the state contest for his essay on race. Miss Purchase read the essay in assembly because James, who was born with a raw purple birthmark covering half of his face, refused to get up in front of the school. His essay was about the birthmark, and it began—I remember this clearly because when Miss Purchase read the first sentence, I felt a sob gathering in my stomach, charging upward, and I was afraid I'd have to leave the assembly—"I was born dirty, and so I think I know how it feels to be born black."

I remember looking down at my hands and thinking, Are these the hands of a black girl, and are they dirty?

That night I told my mother. She said exactly what I wanted to hear, what she had always said on the subject of race when it came to her children, that I was black and white, and lucky for that, with two histories, two cultures, a richer blood to carry into the world. I believed her.

Sex was the next decision I was asked to make at this university. Not whether or not to have it, or when, or under what circumstances. But with whom. And not in terms of an individual but in terms of a group.

I had to make a declaration of sexual preference. To take a stand.

It seems to me such a decision alters the brain the way drugs do. You lose the capacity to know through exploration, to understand beneath the surface of the skin, to know your own self, not in the company of witnesses but alone.

I know something about sex, although my actual experience has been imaginary. But there've been imaginary experiences, as constant and out of my direct control as the regular flow of blood.

At the time of my first "purple thought"—that's Caroline's expression for sexual memory—I was seven and happily involved in several intense love affairs. With Jesus first, whose insipid pale, bearded, blue-eyed, non-Semitic picture I carried in the front flap of my bookbag and kissed good night before I put him to sleep under my pillow. And then I lay with waking dreams of Ms. Printemps, my second-grade music teacher, a crabby woman in her thirties with a high French voice. I don't know why I loved her so, but there she was, beside me in my single bed, our bodies touching from head to toe, although standing she was twice my height.

By day, I loved a man in his early fifties called Ape—even by himself, in honor of his large and hairy body—who owned the store at the corner of our street. I stopped there every day on my way to school to buy a Tootsie Pop. I never spoke to Ape, but he spoke to me, and he must have known by the way my face burned and the breath went out of me when I saw him.

"How's my favorite little nigger girl, this a.m.?" He'd smile a sun-wide smile.

I loved that a black man on the corner of our white block, the only black man I knew, called me nigger—an endearment, an intimacy between us, because we were known to each other.

For a while, I actually thought he might be my father, sticking close so he could watch me grow up in the shadow of my mama's house, where John Taylor's name was mud, according to Aunt Winona.

When I got older, I pretended that he *was* my father.

My only normal boyfriend, real and my own age, was Sergei Andropov, from Georgia, in the Soviet Union, who had escaped with his parents before *glasnost* and come to St. Louis to live with a relative. He refused to learn to speak English, although he read and wrote well enough to get a Satisfactory in second grade.

His assigned seat was one to the right and one ahead of me, so I could examine him in complete secrecy, memorize his hands, his feet, the tufts of beigey hair, the square jaw, the occasional tremor in his chin.

I liked that he refused to speak English, as if it were testament to our love affair, a consummate act of loyalty, that he would communicate with no one.

I am a virgin. It is difficult to separate my imagination from the facts of my life, since I am by nature interior and sometimes the boundaries that separate the mind from the realities of the exterior world are fuzzy.

In my mind, I am always going to sleep making love to someone—a man or a woman or a boy or Jesus, someone whose name I know, although our nighttime intimacy is concealed by the light of day.

So there are things I know even as a virgin. But not enough to act on daydreams.

The sexual mandate came the day after I had been asked to make a choice on race.

I sat down for lunch at a table with a group of girls, choosing them because there were no men, and because I am self-conscious, because I have difficulty eating in the company of men.

The girl next to me was red-haired, squarish, a girl someone of my mother's generation would call cute. She turned to me with the most engaging smile and said in a normal voice:

"Do you like pussy?"

I had no chance to organize my defenses.

The girl next to her laughed. "You're so outrageous, Joanie."

"Cut to the chase," the redhead named Joanie said. "I have too much work to waste my time."

"Don't worry about Joanie," the girl across from me said, one of those beautiful girls I mentioned earlier, in a tiny flowered dress with no flesh in evidence. "She's a cupcake."

The same beautiful girl called my dormitory that evening and asked me to come out for coffee. I said no, using the bronchitis excuse, so she came over to my room, lay down on my bed, and said that Joanie was impossible, her mind forever in the sewer. Everyone in their group at the lunch table was wondering—and so she'd been elected to ask— whether I was a lesbian.

"Lesbians and gays are active here, and the word got out that you would like to join," she said.

Her name was Daphne and she said she was from Hartford and she herself had known since her first crush, on her third-grade teacher. So I thought about Ms. Printemps, and not just her but Lani Sailor and Jamie O'Brien as well, and said I didn't know whether I was a lesbian or not.

It was true. Everything seemed possible at the moment.

Repressed Anxiety Syndrome, Winona calls my constant indecision, although the anxiety is not necessarily repressed.

Daphne told me that I'd find myself falling into groups at college, that it would be necessary to join something. For her part, she was grateful for her association with gays and lesbians. She believed in the political role her group was taking in eliminating discrimination based on sexual preference.

Besides, she said smiling, she loved women.

"Let us know. Come to dinner tomorrow night."

"Thanks," I replied.

"You probably *do* know," Daphne said, touching my hair. "It's just hard to come to terms, especially for people growing up in the Middle West. I know." She laughed. "My mother is from Nebraska."

The infirmary at this university dispenses inhalers. They are small aerosol containers with medication that you spray in your throat, and the medication—no doubt containing carcinogenic chemicals—opens up your airways. On my first day of classes, I noticed that a number of students had these inhalers, and once or twice saw someone use one during class.

"Do you use an inhaler?" a young man sitting next to me in chemistry asked.

I shook my head.

"Mostly women use them, I've noticed," he said. "My girlfriend says it's because the environment is so polluted. Soon we'll be wearing gas masks out of doors." He shrugged. "I think it's PMS."

After class, I called Jacob to ask him did he know about inhalers.

By that evening, I had gone to the infirmary with difficulty breathing. The nurse on duty gave me an inhaler with instructions.

"Do you think it's the environment?" I asked.

"Who knows?" she asked, raising her eyebrows. "I suppose it's stress."

It was stress that sent me to the infirmary.

There was a note from Daphne in my mailbox saying she hoped to see me that evening.

"Take heart," she wrote.

When I came home from the infirmary with my inhaler, Daphne was on the machine.

"See you soon," she said cheerfully.

I punched Pause, then Rewind. And climbed into bed.

I don't know anything about real romance. In my dreams, I'm indiscriminate. I can't imagine a real flesh-and-blood person in my room. I can't imagine taking off my clothes or lying naked alongside another human being, man or woman. I'm not ready for that responsibility. I am not ready.

I daydream of flowers. Especially dahlias. When I was very young, at the beginning of memory, when what I knew of childhood was a series of still lifes, disconnected from the narrative of my life, Mama and I made a garden in the tiny triangle behind our house.

The day is clear and we are kneeling in the damp grass, the smell more must than grass, crumbling the dirt, putting seeds in the earth. I love the smell of gardening, the woolly smell of my mother's sweater. I kiss her hand.

"My hand is dirty, Lilly," she says—this was before I called myself Sage.

"We named you for lilies of the valley," my mother says to me—for the pure white dancing bells that dip lighthearted in late May against the green wings of their leaves. But I know I'm named for my Methodist grandmother, my mother's repressed, unhappy mother.

We must have filled the earth with seeds that spring—and I wonder how my mother, a woman with so many children, a student of medicine, had the time for a garden.

But that is what we did, and what gave me particular joy were the dahlias. I can still see them— late-summer dahlias with wide round faces of brilliant petals, like the petals of a child's drawing of flowers in their perfect stillness.

My mother cuts one, with only a small stem so the crimson dahlia fills my palm.

If I close my eyes now, I am transported on my own green wings from this dormitory room violated by the arrival of Steven Carney banging on my bedroom door, a crimson dahlia the size of a child's palm pressed against my eyes, blocking the invasion of light.

Chapter Six

The hall outside my room is full of the early-morning sounds of growly undergraduates, up half the night, now late for class. It's unlikely that Steven Carney is still outside my door. Someone would notice him and ask what he, a stranger, has in mind sitting on the floor beside room A426.

He's probably gone to get coffee and a bagel, to smoke a cigarette and read the newspaper, waiting until Emerson Hall is empty of students off to labs and lectures for the day. By ten o'clock this morning, it will be just me and Steven Carney, who'll figure that by that hour he can come back unobserved. The manic-depressive down the hall will be in bed. He's in his depressive cycle at the moment and tends not to leave his room. I know this because he's a friend, so to speak, which means we do speak but that's all. I like him. He's the only person I've met here so far who wouldn't bolt if he happened to stumble across my Fear List.

Since last December, my Fear List is no longer a secret. Even Aunt Winona knows. Emmy was searching my room for weed or contraceptives and found the Fear List in my underwear drawer and told Mama, who told Winona.

"I can't help it, Sage. I had to tell," Emmy said. "Admit it. It's a little weird to be afraid of so many things."

I narrowed my eyes at her. I have great eyes. They can scare a person half to death, and I have a look which does just that, especially with my family.

"Sometimes I don't know what's up with you," Emmy told me. "You never talk about the personal stuff."

I don't talk about the personal stuff because there isn't any. Until Steven Carney, nothing was up with me at all. Zilcho. From the age of zero to eighteen. Not even a kiss.

"Do you want me to show you where I keep my birth control pills?" I asked.

"Don't be crazy," Emmy replied. "Of course not."

I'm not crazy, but Aunt Winona likes to think I am. It gives her a sense of purpose, a feeling of control. So when Emmy found my Fear List and told Mama, and Mama told Winona, Winona decided I was having Acute Separation Anxiety.

From her professional point of view, the problem was complicated by my position as the last child in a dysfunctional family.

It was January of my senior year in high school and I was upstairs in my room studying for midterms when I overheard their conversation coming through the heat register. It was the mention of dysfunctional family that got to Mama.

"We're not dysfunctional, Winona," my mother said in a cucumber voice. "We function very well."

"Of course you do, Louisa."

Winona's the older sister and condescending by nature—a quality I discovered during my perilous years as a high school student to be associated with people of limited imagination.

"But you know what I mean," Winona went on.

"No," my mother said. "I don't know what you mean."

"You're a single mother raising biracial children in the nineties," Winona said in a tone of self-congratulation, as if her observation were a discovery.

"It's a wonder all of your patients aren't dead by their own hand," my mother said, her voice dropping underground.

This sent Winona into a rage. Suicide prevention is her badge of honor.

"Never a suicide," she will say, with a prideful clicking sound at the front of her tongue. "Not one suicide in all my years of practice."

Winona is tall like my mother, with pale red hair and a softness about her. The look probably works well enough for therapy when the patients can imagine Winona to be their own mother. But in general, she's awfully stupid about people. She counts on memorizing definitions of human neuroses, at which she really is quite good, to qualify her as an expert on the workings of the human heart.

I heard her temper sizzling: a hiss whooshing right up the heat register. A "Fuck you," which was a first from Aunt Winona, who does not swear. And then a full-blown conflagration.

"I'm glad I'm not your daughter, Louisa," she said. "And I'm certainly glad I'm not half black."

My mother put the house up for sale the following day.

We lived in a duplex on Moran Street in North County; Aunt Winona lived in the other half. We'd been here since my mother moved from the place on T Street in Washington, and it had been good to live next door to kin. Mostly, to be honest—you understand I like her in the abstract—Winona had been helpful to my mother and to us. So it was news to me that she was a racist.

All these years I'd thought we were the apple of Winona's eye, her beloved flesh and blood, her own imagined babies, closer than kin. And instead, she was wishing us white.

I didn't say anything to Mama, but I did tell Jacob.

"Forget it," he said. "Winona is menopausal."

Menopause is worse with women who've never had babies, he told me. And probably in the case of Winona not even sex—all that good equipment lying useless in her belly's drawer. Think of how jealous she must be of Mama, with five beige babies and years of sex with a stud like my father.

It was the first time Jacob had talked about our father except at the dinner table when everybody else would be talking about him and Jacob would say something stupid fitting an older child, like, "They'd probably get along fine now that we're grown up."

"Tell me about John Taylor," I said to Jacob.

We call our father by his name—John Taylor—

even with each other, as if he were a stranger or an acquaintance or someone we read about in the newspaper.

When our father left, Jacob was ten. I've always imagined that he knew things about John Taylor and, being Jacob, wouldn't talk, wouldn't take the responsibility for his own conversation. I know that feeling. I'm a little like him myself.

"I remember he was black," he said deadpan.

That's a real Jacob Taylor remark.

"Try again," I said.

"Well, you've seen pictures."

"You can't tell about a person from pictures," I said. I had a million questions.

After all, thanks to Aunt Winona's sensitivity, I knew the stunning information that my father had left when my mother refused to abort the fetus that turned out to be me.

"Did he like us?" I asked.

"You weren't born," Jacob said.

"Be serious. I'm assuming if he liked you, he would probably have liked me."

We were sitting in the kitchen watching an agent from Temper Real Estate put up a FOR SALE sign in our front yard. Mama was at work, Jacob had twenty-four hours off psychiatry rotation and was home doing his laundry.

Jacob has blond curly hair, which he wears long-ish, and a broad face with green eyes set wide and deep. On this silver winter afternoon, I noticed a dark cast to his face, a quality of the exotic which comes of mixing races, of John Taylor pressing from beneath the surface of his skin.

Sometimes he seems younger than twenty-nine, because he's tentative and quiet and socially graceless. But this afternoon, he had a force, a kind of assurance. I believed what he told me not because he was my older brother but because what he said felt true.

"John Taylor was like you," he said.

"Like me?"

"Quite a lot."

Like me, I thought, the breath gone from my lungs.

The sun spilled into the room and over my trembling hands. I got up and went to the window, making some remark about the FOR SALE sign to diffuse the heat of the moment.

My father was like me. He is like me. We are secret partners, out of the same black seed, two souls split open on the table of chance, separated by accident before we had an opportunity to test the temperature.

"He's quiet," Jacob was saying, "and concealed like you, with a sort of ho-hum, off-the-back-burner, soft humor. Very smart. We used to laugh a lot."

This news pleased me more than I could say.

"It's strange, isn't it," Jacob went on. "A person is born with an actual temperament, like eye color—so you are who you are, which in your case happens to be like your father, even though you never knew him."

Jacob looked at me with real affection, as if we had crossed into a new geography and he suddenly saw me for the first time.

"Was he tall?" I asked, changing the thrust of the conversation to matters of detail, not able to tolerate the emotional richness of the moment.

I had always thought of John Taylor as tall. He looked tall in the pictures. But there was a reason for me to wonder about his height, because I'm not tall.

We go like this: Jacob, six-two; Emmy, five-eleven; Tobias, five-ten-and-a-half; Caroline, five-ten; Mama, five-nine; and me, five-two—not tall enough to feel like a player in this family.

So I guessed my father was not tall, and I was right.

"He used to call me Potboiler," Jacob said.

There was something in the way Jacob said it, some weight or intimacy, that sent me later, after he left with his laundry, on a mission to his old room, to find what secrets he might have hidden there—and Jacob was a person I had never suspected of secrets, too practical by nature, too controlled to allow an interior life.

"What did he mean by 'Potboiler'?" I asked.

"It's a book in which something is always about to happen," he said. "I love the name, but it doesn't exactly suit the person I turned out to be. You know what else I remember," he added. "He used to call Mama 'Clip-Clop.' "

"Clip-Clop?" I laughed. "What in the world does that mean?"

"Who knows?" he said. "It was personal."

"And you never asked?"

"Ask Mama about John Taylor?" He smiled. "Are you crazy?"

That was my clue. Real clue, that is, not like the scarlet romance of Emmy's stories of our parents' love affair, or our father's furtive escape from a life of responsibility, this man with a paper-doll role in our imaginations. Now he was grounded in my mind for a moment, a real man, like me in temperament, who had the courage, the sense of himself, the humor, to call my explosive, sometimes ferocious mother Clip-Clop.

I had never spent time in Jacob's room before. Certainly I'd never been invited.

When Tobias was small, he and Jacob shared a room on the second floor. But as they got older, Tobias was too disorderly, so Jacob moved to the third floor, to a small space next to the attic. It was furnished like a cell, with a desk, a dresser, and a bed, and a picture of our family before my father left and one of Jacob holding me as a baby, fat then, with a curly black cap of hair and a cockeyed smile, brown as the Missouri earth next to his pale beige skin.

In Jacob's desk, I found letters, which I read.

There were several from a girl named Miranda from Northwestern, where he had gone to college, letters breaking up with him in the artificial language of terminal romances—whatever the limitations of my personal experience with romance, I read the slicks. "We'll always be friends," Miranda wrote in the round handwriting of young girls, full of *o*'s—"I'll always love you and admire and respect you."

There were letters from my cousin in Michigan and from my grandmother in St. Louis when she was traveling in California, and Christmas and birthday cards, even some from me. There was nothing that might give me a glimpse into my brother's secret life except an envelope that I found between two confessional letters of sincere regret from Miranda, almost identical in content and absent of any imagination.

The envelope was addressed to Jacob Taylor at a post office box in St. Louis, with a return address of John Taylor, in care of Taylor, at a box in Sunflower, Mississippi, and was postmarked July 8, 1990.

So they had been in touch.

Jacob must have gotten his own post office box in order to receive letters from our father. They could have been writing back and forth for years. It might still be happening.

The letter was written on yellow legal paper in blue ballpoint pen. The handwriting was large and slanted and masculine, and difficult to make out.

Dear Jacob,

I'm here in Sunflower for a couple of weeks, packing up and selling the house where I grew up. My brother, your Uncle Albert, died here this spring, turning over the tractor on himself while he was plowing the field. He was probably drunk. He was often drunk and had lived here alone since our father died, when you were two or three years old.

The house is outside Sunflower about ten miles and before the emancipation belonged to a plantation owner named Taylor from whom we took our name, as happened with slaves. Some of the land in our case and many others' was divided up and distributed to the slaves after they'd been set free.

My mother, who was half white, some Creole, some other blood, from Louisiana, moved here with my father when she was seventeen, and they had four children, two stillbirths and Albert and me. Daddy made the assumption that the stillbirths and Mama's dying early were due to weak genes from being a half-breed, but that's not likely.

Daddy thought of himself as a purebred—pure black, which he wasn't of course, none of us is. But he was the blue-black color of Africa—with that kind of impenetrable black skin which you don't often see in places like St. Louis. And he was extremely proud of it.

So I grew up different from many of the blacks I knew—as good as—better than—proud of—those convictions because of my father.

I'm guessing you maybe don't know that your mother and I loved each other. Our getting together didn't have to do with race or with politics, as happened with a lot of black and white people at the time of the civil rights movement in the south. Or with whether my children would have paler, fairer skin than I had. I didn't love her because she was white. What happened between us happened.

Life has a way of surprising you—the way the world looks at one moment is very different from the way it looks at another. And sometimes, you can't catch hold. Which is what happened to our lives in Washington, D.C.

I am not by nature a sentimental man, but it struck me as I signed the papers last night to sell this house to Mr. and Mrs. Benedict Fowler, black folks from the next county, the place the Taylors have lived in probably since 1830, I ought to remind my children that half the genes in every one of you are mine.

Enclosed are pictures of my parents, your grandparents, Uncle Albert, and me, and the place where we grew up. Save them.

Love, Pa

I folded the letter, slid it under my shirt as I went downstairs, in case Jacob or Aunt Winona or even Mama might be sitting at the end of my bed waiting for me.

Then, out of breath with excitement, I went into my bedroom, closed the door, and put the letter into a shoe box at the back of my closet, where I had moved my Fear List and where I packed the treasures of my life which I had brought with me when I came to school in September.

That was last winter, more than nine months ago. I didn't ask Jacob about the letter. I didn't want him to know I'd been through his things, although if he didn't want anyone to know, he shouldn't have left evidence. I don't even know why I felt it was urgent to look through his drawers, which is more something Emmy would do.

But I must have expected to find something. I

think you look for things when you're ready to find them.

I finished high school and went to Martha's Vineyard and things started with Steven Carney and then the awful stuff I haven't mentioned yet that happened at the end of August, so I forgot. But when Jacob came to put me in college in September, I asked him did he think our father was dead.

"No," he said. "I don't."

"How come?" I wondered whether they were still in contact. The letter I had found was more than five years old.

"I just don't." He wasn't going to say any more.

By the alarm clock it's almost ten-thirty, and Steven Carney is back. He's trying to open my door now, pushing against it with the force of his body, rattling the knob. There's no place to hide in this tiny room, so I crawl under the bed. It's a wonder that I fit, big as I am. I keep my dirty laundry under the bed and there's a lot of it, so I scrunch over to the wall and fill the space between me and the room with laundry.

If he does get in, which, by the sound of it, he's going to, he'll think I've bolted.

Chapter Seven

My parents had a house on Duncan Street in Jackson called Halfway Home. They started the place for people in trouble, mostly black teenagers, but there were also some battered women, their children, and alcoholic men. They could stay as long as three months, long enough to get their lives together with Louisa and John Taylor's help. According to Mama, the place was always full.

We have a picture of it on the wall of our kitchen

on Moran Street: a big falling-down house with a
porch crowded with young women and children.
Jacob holds Caroline in the picture, and Mama's
there in the middle, her arms slung over the shoulders of two young women.

The picture I have of Halfway Home in the shoe
box I brought from St. Louis is similar. It's summer
and the porch is full of people, but in this picture,
John Taylor is there with Emmy, and Mama, holding Caroline, is in the left-hand corner. Mama's
wearing overalls, and a bandanna around her head,
and she looks adorable, like a girl, as I've never seen
her.

On the back is written: *July 18, 1970, the day
Venus came to live at Halfway Home.*

We all know about Venus. Hers is one of those
stories that get kept. But I've never seen a picture
of her, and I probably never will. In this one, she
has her back full to the camera, her hip stuck out,
her arms folded overtop her head, vamping. And
she's only seven years old.

What I know about Venus is that she came off
the street; she was the child of a prostitute, who
tried to kill her by pushing her into the river. By
some kind of miracle, Venus swam. She was the
only person to stay at Halfway Home beyond three
months. She stayed four years, and died there, and
that was the end of my parents' experiment in hu-
manity.

They closed the house the week following her death and moved to Washington. I have a copy of a feature article from a magazine about it. We all have copies.

At Halfway Home, my parents lived in a cottage behind the main house, a two-room cottage with a front porch and an outhouse, which seemed to please Mama and upset her Methodist parents—the thought of their daughter, pregnant, peeing down a dark hole in the middle of the night, walking barefoot through the cold to do it. My parents lived in one room and their children in the other. Venus slept in the children's room at Mama's insistence.

"I don't like Venus with the babies, Louisa," John Taylor is saying.

They are lying on their bed in the cottage. It's summer, too hot without a fan, their bodies barely touching.

"She's not half civilized," John Taylor says.

"She'll be okay, John," Louisa says. *"We'll civilize her."*

He reaches down and takes her hand. "Some things you can't fix, darling."

"Venus is a child," Louisa says. *"Of course she can be fixed."*

"I don't know about that," John Taylor says.

The sun is falling to the other side of the earth, taking the heat with it, and they lie extremely still.

They are waiting for a breath of coolness to pass across their near-naked bodies, listening for the sounds from the room where Emmy and Jacob and Caroline are sleeping, where Venus has a little bed just under the window.

"You've been a surprise to me, Louisa Taylor," he says.

"A good surprise?" she asks.

"A miracle," John Taylor says, and she slips under his arm, spreads her long red hair like a sheet across his chest, thinking to herself what a flight she has had from St. Louis, what a romantic adventure, witnessing the scene as she lies against her husband. She is not a beautiful woman, but there is a loveliness in her contentment, a sense of rightness about her life, almost like religion.

"But don't let it go to your head." John Taylor laughs, kissing her baby-stretched belly, her soft lips.

Caroline's animal cries wake them, and they are out of bed, pulling on their clothes. They run through the door to the porch and through the door off the porch to the children's room, where they can see, in the moonlight, Venus standing over Caroline's crib, striking out at her, and Jacob on Venus's back like a monkey, biting and biting her.

It is almost dawn when they lie back down on the bed in their room—no longer alone—Caroline between them, sleeping now, her fist stuffed in her mouth, Jacob and Emmy wrapped together at the bottom of the bed. Venus, without remorse, sleeps in her small bed under the window of the children's room.

"Venus is mean," Jacob says.

"Right," Emmy agrees. "She has a knife."

"An eating knife, not a sharp one," Louisa says.

"Sharp enough to cut," Jacob says.

Which she has done—there are tiny cuts on Caroline's arms and across her belly, made with a dull-edged silverplated knife.

"I have taken the knife away," Louisa says.

"I want you to take Venus away," Emmy says.

After the children have fallen asleep, John Taylor reaches over and takes Louisa's hand. "Darling?"

"Don't touch me." Louisa rolls over on her side, away from him. "I don't want to be touched."

The article from a September 1974 *Time*, which I keep in the shoe box, has a few stories on the current whereabouts of 1960s freedom workers in Mississippi. There is a picture of Louisa and John Taylor in front of 33 Duncan Street, with the sign HALFWAY HOME over the porch. There are no children, just the two of them looking gloomy and an ugly yellow dog.

"John and Louisa Taylor in front of Halfway Home the week after Venus hanged herself," the caption reads. There is a paragraph in the article about Venus and the house and what the Taylors were trying to do there and couldn't.

"It didn't work," Louisa is quoted as saying.

"It worked," John Taylor says in the article. "It just didn't save Venus."

Good-bye, Mississippi, September 28, 1974

The picture that comes next in my parents' lives was taken in front of the house on Duncan Street when they were packing up. Jacob sits on the hood of a long Chevrolet, and Emmy is coming out of the house with a small suitcase, and Mama, very pregnant with Tobias, leans against the car with the ugly yellow dog at her feet.

We didn't have many conversations about Mama's life in Mississippi, but we knew about Venus, and one night when we were all at the dinner table, Emmy asked why she'd hanged herself.

"She wanted to," Mama said.

We didn't ask her why. It was too awful the way Mama said it, so we sat quietly around the table— you could almost hear our breathing—until finally Tobias spoke.

"Where?" he asked.

"In the kitchen," Mama said.

When we went through the boxes in the house on Moran Street, where I grew up, we didn't find many pictures taken in Washington, D.C. None of me, of course, so when we divided them, I got only one, which, according to Tobias, is the first picture ever taken of me.

After Christmas, 1977. Winter Doldrums

Mama doesn't look pregnant in this photograph, but she must have been, because I was born several months later. The picture is bathed in light, slightly overexposed; she is lying on a couch in a red robe, her hair in braids, with what appears to be a crown sitting cockeyed across her forehead like a joke. My father is leaning against the wall in a posture of conversation, his arm extended toward Mama. The ugly yellow dog is lying on my mother's feet. We have never had a dog in St.

Louis, so the animal passion must have belonged to my father.

The pictures from Washington that my brothers and sisters got are of birthday parties and Christmas mornings and Easter egg hunts. I believe I have been given the picture of the end of my parents' marriage.

"Think about it, Louisa," John Taylor is saying. "I'm a civil rights commissioner making a small salary, living in a rowhouse on a drug corner with four young children."

"And a pregnant wife," Louisa says.

"I can't handle another child, Louisa," he says. "We can't."

"I can," Louisa says.

He folds his arms across his chest and paces the living room. In another room Jacob and Emmy are fighting, and he shouts for them to shut up.

"That's very nice, John," Louisa says, laying her arm over her eyes to keep out the light of day. " 'Shut up' are not words I'm anxious for my children to know."

"Our children," he says.

He gets a cup of coffee from the kitchen, and spills some on his shirt because his hand is shaking. He asks Louisa does she want coffee, and she does not.

"It's my choice whether to stay pregnant or not," she says.

"Yes, it's your choice," he agrees, sliding into a chair next to the couch, putting his feet on the coffee table.

"You can leave if it's too much for you," she says.

"I won't leave," he says.

"Then you've got to understand I won't have an abortion," Louisa says. "It's not even a subject of conversation."

"I understand," John says.

"You believe I'll change my mind, don't you," she says.

"No I don't," John says wearily. "I have no reason to believe you ever change your mind."

"Well, I won't," she says. "So if you have to leave, go."

Aunt Winona likes to cause trouble. When she told me that my father had left because my mother refused to abort me, I believed her. It was easy to think of my father as a villain, since I'd never seen him.

When Emmy had an abortion, I didn't think about the baby as a life. I don't think of Maggie as her second child, as if Maggie had a sibling who died.

On the subject of my own life, rescued by my

mother from certain oblivion, I have only a vague sense of vulnerability, of a life hung in the balance, almost dispensed with. But that sense of myself didn't exactly feel like my life until lately.

I do feel accountable for John Taylor's leaving.

I sometimes wish he could see me. Not as I am now but as I'd like to be, as I dream of being. I imagine our meeting. I'm tall and beautiful and married, with a fine berry-brown son named John Jefferson and a reputation as an excellent physician. My father is extraordinarily proud of me.

The telephone has been ringing, and my organic chemistry professor is speaking to the answering machine. She is unpleasant, and I wish I could get out from under this bed and turn off her voice so I wouldn't have to listen to it. But Steven Carney is still trying to get the door open, and I'm going to stay right here behind the laundry, for days if necessary.

"Ms. Taylor," she's saying in that terrible voice which made it hard for me to remain in her class. "I have told the dean you haven't been in class for some time and you haven't returned my calls. I have suggested that she contact your family."

Someone has just come into my room. I don't hear anything, but I can tell there has been a change in the light along the floor, as if the door had opened and shadows of darkness had flooded in. I lie very still and hold my breath. Stuffed into the corner under my bed, I imagine Venus hanging in the kitchen of Halfway Home. I can't get her out of my mind.

C h a p t e r   E i g h t

W hen the call came from the dean, Emmy Taylor was vacuuming the living room rug. She turned the switch off, stepped over the boxy Hoover, and grabbed the phone.

"Hello," she said, out of breath.

The dean introduced herself, but before she had a chance to say another word, Emmy knew something had happened to Sage. Something terrible was in the weather for the Taylor family this year.

In a voice wafer-thin, her heart flown out of her on wings, she said—later she could scarcely believe she had—"Is Sage dead?"

The dean, taken aback, defensive as if she'd been accused, replied that no, Sage wasn't dead. She hadn't seen Sage, had never even met her. Was there reason to believe something had happened to her?

"Thank God," Emmy said. "I'm sorry to be unstuck like this. We've had so hard a year."

The dean had called to report that Sage was not attending classes.

"Not going to classes." Emmy sank into the couch, breathless with relief. "Are you sure she's not going to classes? I talked to her last night and she told me what happened yesterday in chemistry lab, and about a paper she's writing for African-American lit." Emmy held the baby in her arms and tried to pull the edge of the rug out of the mouth of her new curly-coated retriever puppy, but he wouldn't have it, shaking his head, biting her finger with his needle-point teeth.

"I'm sorry," Emmy said. "I have a new puppy." She could have gone on and on about the puppy and Maggie and being out of milk—but she stopped herself.

"Sage called about ten last night. She'd just come back from the library. And she called again this morning, at eight forty-five."

"I see." The dean had one of those administrator voices, delivering all news without measurement, the sound of her voice traveling on the telephone wire like blame.

Emmy wanted to shout at her, "Sage is just a young girl who's had a hard time, so you be good to her or I'll wring your neck."

"I have called her room twice in the last week, after I received Failure to Attend Class notes from her professors," the dean said. "I left a message on her machine asking her to be in touch with me."

The baby had begun to whimper.

"Does she have any friends at school that you know of?" the dean asked.

"She does." Emmy tried to remember the people Sage had mentioned. But so much had happened in her own life—the baby's virus, and the new puppy peeing his little heart out on the living room rug, and Mama, always Mama.

"Do you know their names?"

"She's mentioned Paulette and Allie and Fan. I don't know the last names. She has a boyfriend." When they had last talked, Sage had made a point of telling Emmy that a boy named Paul—she called him Saint Paul—had told her she had a smile like the rising sun, and called her Shine. "I don't know any more about him than the name Paul."

"She isn't in her room," the dean said. "We had Security check at around ten this morning."

"You opened the door? You had a policeman open the door? That's her private room." Emmy was emotional in her daily life, unlike her absolute and orderly mother, unlike Caroline. "Doesn't she pay for that room and have a lock?"

"She hasn't been seen, Ms. Taylor," the dean said in a voice of artificial patience. "We are concerned."

"And what did you find when you went in her room?" Emily asked.

"The room was neat except for laundry under the bed. That's what the security guards reported. I wasn't there."

"Sage is always neat. She was making her bed by the time she was five."

"Well, I don't have anything more to add," the dean said. "She hasn't been in her classes, and she doesn't return my calls. I don't believe she'll be able to finish the semester even if she goes back to classes tomorrow. What do you suggest?"

Emmy didn't know what to say. She wished she knew Sage. She wished she understood what went on in that sweet and complicated brain.

"It's hard to be the youngest," Tobias had once said about Sage. "You're always knowing the older ones because you pay attention and no one is knowing you." And he was right. None of them really knew Sage except perhaps Tobias.

"In spite of your reservations, I'll have Security

check the room more thoroughly," the dean was saying. "If you've talked to her, she must be someplace."

Emmy had a sudden mental picture of her little sister sitting in the back of her closet or under her bed, wrapped in the blue stadium blanket from their mother's bed, a child in hiding. DO NOT DISTURB.

"So far this year," the dean continued triumphantly, "Sage has missed four papers, a quiz in African-American literature, two exams in chemistry lab, and all of her labs in invertebrate biology. She hasn't attended any class since the first week of school."

"Don't search her room," Emmy said. "I'll call my sister Caroline in Philadelphia to see if Sage is there, and then I'll call you back."

"One other thing," the dean said, her trump card, her thin knife against the middle of Emmy's back. "You are Sage's guardian? That's what I have listed here."

"I'm not her guardian. Sage is an adult. I'm her older sister."

"Your parents are divorced?"

Her parents weren't divorced. There had been no formal papers, no conversations, no lawyers, no legal separation. Her father had been asked to leave when Emmy was thirteen and their mother was pregnant with Sage. And he had gone. Now married, a mother herself, understanding better the nature of relationships between men and women, Emmy guessed her mother had longed for her father to say, "No, I won't leave. I'll stay with you forever." But her father, burdened by the responsibility of too many children, confused by the heat of Louisa's wrath, had left, hoping she would come after him, would call or send a letter, would be lonely without him and change her mind.

That was nineteen years ago. Her mother had sustained an anger as fresh as a new injury, enraged at the mention of John Taylor, at any question of communication with him on the part of her children, at any sign of affection. Any interest in his whereabouts was an act of disloyalty toward her family. Although in every other way, Dr. Louisa Taylor had been a reasonable woman, a scientist, rational to a fault.

But the power of Louisa's feelings toward John Taylor could not have lasted unabated unless the coin of their love affair was easily reversible. If the possibility had been there, they would have reunited with the same passion that split them apart.

There was no reasoning with Mama.

"My parents aren't divorced," Emmy said.

Surely this dean knew about Mama, she thought. But maybe not, so Emmy didn't bring it up.

"They're unavailable," she added. "I'll call you back when I talk to my sister in Philadelphia."

She hung up the phone, put the baby in her carriage, rocked it with her foot, took her brown suede clog from the puppy and put it on, then dialed Caroline's studio.

Caroline's place on Cherry Street had a living room and a bedroom, but she called it her studio and continued to paint there even after Tobias moved in and turned the place into a marijuana den.

"Rabbits," Caroline said when she picked up the phone. "Rabbits. Rabbits. Rabbits."

"Caroline."

"Hi, Em. What if I told you I was pregnant?"

"I'm not in a good mood," Emmy said, sitting on the floor with the puppy. "We have a problem."

"*You* have a problem. I said 'rabbits' for the first day of the month so I have no problems, only good luck."

Caroline didn't like to hear about problems or bad news, even when things happened to people she didn't know. She seldom read the newspapers, and never the metro section with its reports of local tragedies. Like her mother, she was focused and orderly, defended by work, ill equipped for feelings out of her control; she rode over trouble as if it didn't exist, as if her slice of the world were always sunny.

"The dean at Sage's school has called," Emmy said. "She says that Sage isn't going to classes."

"I just talked to Sage a while ago. Eight this morning, she called. She was about to go running, and then she had a class. Five miles, she's running every day or so."

"Did she call you for a reason?"

"She calls every day," Caroline said. "Doesn't she call you every day?"

"Sometimes twice."

"She called to say what was up. She has a boyfriend and she got an A on a paper in Afro studies and a hundred on a calculus quiz. That sort of stuff. She seems good."

"She's not going to school," Emmy said.

"What do you mean, she's not going to school?"

"Just that."

"Sage doesn't lie," Caroline said. "She's secretive, but you know she doesn't lie."

"She didn't use to. But now apparently she's lying to us about school."

"What's she doing, then?" Caroline asked. "She must be doing something."

"I don't know what she's doing," Emmy said. "I just know she's not going to school."

"She says she is, Em. We're her sisters. We ought to believe her."

"They keep roll. Not everyone at that university can be wrong."

Caroline hesitated. "I've got to get some coffee." She put the phone down, and Emmy could hear the dishes rattling, Tobias's voice rambling, and music in the background. When Caroline came back to the phone, her tone was flat. "Maybe we should call Jacob," she said.

"Have him paged at the hospital?"

"He's probably in surgery now," Caroline said.

"He'll be out before lunch." She picked up Maggie and burrowed her face in the baby's soft belly.

"I wish we could call Mama," she said.

"Well, we can't," Caroline said. "So don't bother to wish."

After Emmy hung up, Caroline dialed Sage's number. She was worried, but she had not let Emmy know that. Emmy trusted in Caroline's high spirits and steely nerves, believing her maybe a little less sensitive than the rest of the Taylors, more driven, more selfish perhaps.

Only Sage had a sense of the long black ribbon of sadness in Caroline's heart.

The phone rang six times before Sage's soft and tentative voice came on: "Hello, this is Sage. I'm not here right now. Please leave a message and I'll get back to you." There was a pause. "Soon."

Caroline dialed again and listened to the message, the phone pressed hard to her ear. Something in the "soon," something in the quiet, desperate sound of the word, gave her a terror in her bones, a powerful intuition that Sage was dead.

"Tobias."

Tobias was sleeping. He was always sleeping, usually on the futon on the floor, but today he was sleeping on a hammock on the tiny screened porch overlooking Cherry Street.

"Tobias." Caroline kicked him with her bare foot.

His eyes fluttered but he didn't move.

"Would you wake up for chrissake and join the late twentieth century."

"Shut up, Caroline," Tobias said, without opening his eyes. "I like it best when you're like Mama, cool under pressure. Paint a picture. Do a still life of me sleeping on your hammock. Be sure to get my cleft."

"Go live with Jacob." Caroline shook her brother by the shoulders. "He'll be able to give you a detailed scientific account of how you're frying your brain."

She went back inside and called Barnes Hospital.

"I'd like to page Dr. Jacob Taylor," she said when the receptionist answered. "Tell him to call his sister Caroline in Philadelphia. It's an emergency."

Jacob's probably deep into the open belly of some accident victim, but who cares, she thought. If she didn't say it was an emergency, the receptionist might wait hours before she paged him, and then he'd be at lunch or in class.

She telephoned Sage again and hung up as the machine answered.

When Tobias came in, Caroline was sitting on the futon, her arms wrapped around her legs. He sat down next to her and put his long-fingered hand on hers.

"I'm sorry," he said.

"What's to be sorry for?" she said fiercely. "It's not your fault something has happened to Sage."

"What's happened to Sage?"

"Something. We don't know yet." Caroline folded her arms tight across her chest. "Emmy called because the dean called her."

"I heard."

"Then why did you ask?"

Tobias leaned against the wall and closed his eyes. "I didn't want to hear."

"Would you do me a favor, Tobias? Just this once. Just today."

"Sure." He took out a cigarette.

"Don't do that."

"Smoke?"

"Right. Don't do that, or any weed either, until we find out what's happened to Sage."

Tobias stretched his legs, shook his hair out of his eyes.

"Okay." He put his cigarettes away. "Okay. I'll do that. Now what?"

"We're waiting for Emmy to call back," Caroline said. "She's thinking what we should do."

"We should go to Connecticut."

"That's what I think."

"We can get on a train now."

"I'll call Emmy." Caroline got up too quickly, lightheaded.

"Don't freak," Tobias told her.

"I never freak," she replied.

It occurred to Tobias that he ought to take a shower. Caroline would be pleased if he cleaned up, looked decent, put together, as she'd say. It would give her a sense of confidence.

"I talked to Sage this morning," Caroline said, "and it's still morning. What can happen in so short a time?"

"You're right," Tobias said. "Nothing can happen."

Before Caroline could get to the phone, Emmy called. "The dean wasn't there," she said, "but I left a message that Sage is at your house. I don't want them to send Security into her room, looking in the closets and under the bed. I couldn't stand it."

"We should go there and find Sage ourselves," Caroline said.

"That's what I think," Emmy agreed.

"Tobias and I will take a train."

"But you should wait till we hear from Jacob. And then I'll get a train from Boston and meet you there."

"I want to go soon," Caroline said.

"We will. This isn't like Sage, is it? She's always done school even if she's sort of backward socially."

"It's not like her to say she's doing something she's not," Caroline said. "But who knows?"

"Do you think it's about Mama?" Emmy asked.

"Maybe. Probably. Why pretend? Of course it's about Mama."

"I think so too."

"And she's probably told no one at school," Caroline said.

"She keeps too many secrets." Emmy was wistful, and in spite of Caroline's feelings about their father, she added, "It would be nice if we could find John Taylor."

"What good would that do us?" Caroline asked.

"It would just be nice if we could call him wherever he is and ask him to come take care of Sage," Emmy said.

"Fat chance of that."

Caroline hung up and put away the paints, the scissors, the sketch pad—her intended work for the day. She cleared the breakfast dishes and checked her closet for clean clothes. She had the reputation in the family for action: Emmy talked and Jacob examined points of view and Tobias slept and Sage didn't count yet. But Caroline took action. That's why the others thought she was less sensitive than they. Like Mama. As if Mama hadn't been sensitive to breaking.

Chapter Nine

Daphne is calling—the one I told you is waiting for me to make a decision on sexual preference. She's already called once this week to invite me to a poetry slam at a coffeehouse, and now she's asking how I am and why she never sees me and have I dropped chemistry since we're in the same class and she knows I haven't been attending.

I'm thinking of changing the message on my answering machine to something like, "This is Sage, please hang up when you hear the beep."

"Call if you get this message," Daphne is saying. She repeats her telephone number.

I like the sound of Daphne's voice. It's like Mama's—low and full and warm. When she hangs up, I replay the message pretending that it is Mama speaking, which is easy to do because I imagine the words she's speaking as if they'd been said in another language, listening only to the sound.

Caroline reminds me of Mama because she's matter-of-fact and reliable in an uncomplicated way. But Caroline has a bad voice. It's high and raspy, and it gets on my nerves. Still, I love talking to Caroline because she's dependable, surprisingly for an artist—unlike me, and Emmy, who has the sort of abstracted temperament to cross a street without looking.

We are a close family. Some of my friends, especially Jessica, say "too close for comfort," but it's not exactly true. We're too different from one another to be that close, except Tobias and me, who match: close when we were small, stuck together for eternity, like characters in a book. The rest of us have a sense of one another and love and loyalty, but we don't know one another in the marrow. This probably comes from having different histories, which never could have lined up right—even if Mama and John Taylor had stayed together.

When we were dividing up my father's letters this summer, I found an envelope with Mama's handwriting, to John Taylor but without an address. I put it in among my group of letters without telling anyone. The trouble with being the youngest is that you have last choice in everything; you get what's left over, handed down. Sometimes you have to learn deception.

I took the envelope without telling Jacob, who was in charge of dividing my father's things, and so much happened that I didn't read it until I got stuck in my room with Steven Carney outside the door.

The envelope was sealed and stamped, and when I opened it, I found the date, July 16, this year, written in Mama's hand across the top.

Dear John,

Today a young couple brought their baby into the heart clinic, and it was clear to me the baby's heart is so damaged it will be a miracle if we can save her. The mother was a pretty white woman and he was a sweet and tender black man. When they left, I fell into a terrible depression. And so this letter.

When you walked out of the house on T

Street with a bag of clothes and books, I was outraged. I loved you. I had taken a risk in marrying a black man. My risk, not yours, I thought. You were lucky to have me. If there was leaving to be done, I should have been the one to do it.

I wanted you to come back and tell me you should never have gone, that you were at fault and I was a saint. Gradually, as the months went on and on, there was no way I could see to be back in touch.

I was wrong.

You should know that I have developed a minor heart condition, probably as a result of the rheumatic fever I had when I was young.

About the children, call or write or see them, if you like.

Love,

Louisa

My heart exploded with unexpected joy. I put the letter back in the envelope and sealed it with Scotch tape. When I get out of this dormitory room and find out where he lives, I plan to mail it to him.

Chapter Ten

J acob Taylor sutured the belly of the appendectomy patient, slipped off his gloves, his coat,
his mask, and washed up. He received the
note from the hospital receptionist when he left the
operating room.

"Call your sister Caroline," the message read.
"Emergency."

He pushed through the swinging doors, ducked
into an office, and picked up the phone.

"That can't be right," he said when Caroline told

him the news. "Sage is fine. She leaves me messages every day on my machine."

"She's not fine," Caroline said. "She's home-sick."

"Homesick? She doesn't say she's homesick when she calls. She seems great. She's doing wonderfully, she tells me. I've been impressed she's so together, under the circumstances."

"She's not so together," Caroline said. "That's the point."

"But she says she is." Jacob slipped into the hardback chair, exhausted. Surgery drained him more than the other rotations. He was too tense, his hands less capable of precision than he had imagined they would be.

"You can't just believe what a person says, Jacob. Not everyone is like you."

"What do you want to do, then?" Jacob asked.

"I want to go check on her myself. I think it's the best thing."

"You may be right," Jacob said. "I'll talk to Emmy and then we'll decide."

In Boston, Emmy answered the phone on the first ring.

"I talked to Caroline," Jacob told her.

"I'm listening."

"Sage hasn't said a word to me about trouble. I'm blown away."

"I know. She's said nothing to me either. It's crazy."

"Caroline says you spoke to the dean."

"I hate the dean. She's not at all helpful," Emmy said. "I just don't know what to do."

Jacob could hear her breathing, the baby fussing just beyond the receiver, the yapping of puppy play.

"Do you think there's any chance of our finding John Taylor to help us?" Emmy's voice was steady, even cool.

"John Taylor?" Jacob asked.

"Our father."

"That's crazy, Emmy. Sage didn't even know him."

"I know. That's the point. I have an instinct."

Emmy had instincts for impending disasters and good news, for weather and romance, for changes in circumstance. Even about their mother she had had an instinct.

"What kind of instinct do you have now?"

"Think of it this way. Sage has no father. I mean, he's as good as dead to her. She's never even seen him, and now she loses Mama."

"So?"

"I can't help it, Jacob. When I feel things, I just feel them," Emmy said. "I think we should find John Taylor."

It was ten a.m. in St. Louis, a slippery gray outside the windows of the hospital, and raining. Jacob sat beside the telephone in the small office next to the waiting room, where the parents of the appendectomy patient were sitting and an elderly woman was openly weeping. He wished he were more rational where his family was concerned. In other people's emergencies he was quick to detach; his family was another story.

He had been the one to find his mother in her office on the pediatric ward. Winona called his apartment on Tuesday, August 20, just after midnight.

"Louisa's not at home," she said in her whisper-of-disaster voice. His mother had not attended the reception for pediatricians at which she'd been asked to make some remarks, had not done her usual rounds at the hospital between four and six, had not come home for dinner or phoned or returned the calls from her answering service.

After Winona's call, Jacob headed for his mother's office. He could already see her there almost exactly as he found her—a long, thin pole of a woman with fading red hair sprinkled with white, pale-skinned and pretty. She was wearing a white starched coat, a stethoscope around her neck, her arms folded on the desk as if she had been speaking to someone in the room when she died.

When Sage and Emmy and Caroline and Tobias arrived the next day, Jacob told them what he had learned, that their mother had had a heart problem for a while.

"Why didn't we know?" Emmy asked.

"I didn't know," Jacob said. "No one knew except her doctor. She didn't want anyone to know."

"Did you know, Sage?" Caroline asked. "You were here alone with Mama all year."

Sage shook her head.

"I suspected," Winona said. "I suspected last winter, but I didn't want to say anything. Louisa would take my head off." She gestured toward the FOR SALE sign, still up in the front yard. "Witness," she said. "I hesitated to say anything, with Louisa's bad temper."

They were sitting in the dining room in Winona's half of the duplex, which she kept dark, the windows shut. The house smelled of age, of old perfume, of the overstuffed chairs and walnut furniture from their grandparents' house.

Sage sat at the table without talking, her hands folded, her full lips thinned to a long line as if she had pulled them at either end.

"I have some expertise on denial," Winona said. "In fact, I did my thesis on—well, alcohol was really my specialty, but I know a lot about denial. Louisa was a professional."

The day was unbearably hot, especially in the closed, airless room, but Sage was trembling uncontrollably. She had taken the blue stadium blanket from her mother's bed and wrapped it around herself.

When Winona brought up the subject of denial,

Sage left, without a word, through the front door.
Jacob found her sitting on the front steps of the
house, looking into the distance.

"Don't worry about me." Sage twisted the blanket in her fingers. "It's not Mama I'm upset about."
She pulled the blanket over her head. "I simply had
to leave the house, before I strangled Winona."

Later Jacob found her in the bathroom. The door
was ajar, the light off, and she was sitting on the
edge of the tub. When he opened the door, she was
visible in the long rectangle of light from the hall.

"Sorry to barge in on you, Sagie," he said.

"Never mind. Come in. I'll leave. I was just sitting here."

She got up and walked past him.

"We were just talking about Mama in the living
room. Winona's not here, so you can come down."

They stood in the half-light between the bathroom and the hall, ill at ease.

"You'll feel better if you talk with us," Jacob
said.

Sage looked at him without expression.

"I don't think so." She sank her chin into her
turtleneck, pulled up high.

"*Separation anxiety,*" Aunt Winona said later. "A
perfectly normal thing at Sage's age."

"Her mother has died," Emmy said. "She's dev-
astated."

"Of course, but she hasn't felt Louisa's death
yet. She's in denial," Winona said. "I'll try to talk to
her."

"Don't," Caroline said.

"But Caroline, I understand adolescent girls,"
Winona replied. "I've had experience."

Jacob went into Sage's room late that night while
everyone else was downstairs talking. She was lying
on her stomach reading *People.*

"Okay?" he asked.

"Fine," she said.

"Do you want to go with me to the funeral
home?"

"To see Mama?"

"To see Mama," Jacob said quietly.

"No." Sage didn't look up from her magazine. "I
don't want to."

Jacob picked up the telephone and dialed Sage's
number. He listened to her voice on the answering
machine, analyzed the sound of it for "mental
health," as Winona would say.

"Please call me at home, Sagie," he said. "I'll be there all afternoon."

He told his supervisor at the hospital he had an intestinal flu and wouldn't be able to complete afternoon classes. When he walked into his apartment, the telephone was ringing, and he ran to get it.

"Jacob, thank God I got you," Caroline said. "Have you called Sage?"

"Yes. She wasn't at home, or else she just isn't answering."

"I talked to Emmy and Tobias. I mean, for what it's worth, talking to Tobias. We all agree we ought to go find her, right away."

"You're right, of course," Jacob said.

"I suppose you know that Emmy has an instinct about John Taylor."

"I do know," Jacob said. "What do you think?"

"I think he walked out," Caroline said. "So why should we try to find him now?"

"For Sage. I mean, that's what Emmy said."

"I don't like it. Besides," Caroline added, "what makes you think we can find him?"

"I could ask Winona," Jacob said.

"Well, that's your business," Caroline said. "Emmy's instincts drive me crazy."

Jacob didn't have to call Winona.

His last letter from John Taylor was dated July

1996, from New York City. He had always kept in touch with his father, since his father left or fled or was thrown out of the house on T Street in Washington. But during those years, out of loyalty to his mother, or inhibition, or fear of the riptides in his own heart, he had never called him, never heard his voice, never tried to find his number from information in Chicago or Sunflower or Jackson or Cleveland or Washington, D.C., or now New York City, the places he had lived in the years since he left.

John Taylor's letters were infrequent but careful, written to be saved, to be shown one day to Jacob's sisters and brother so John Taylor could be known to them.

He told Jacob facts. He was working for welfare reform, now for the Urban League in New York City. He had an apartment on the Upper West Side. He was athletic, still, in his fifties, playing basketball, and active in the community. He was not well-to-do but comfortable. He had money if any of his children needed it.

John Taylor never mentioned Louisa unkindly. On several occasions, he expressed admiration for her hard work and energy and dedication. But in one letter he said he knew the money he sent wasn't enough for college tuition for so many children and that saddened him. Jacob was in medical school then, unaware that John Taylor had ever sent money to his family.

The letters were uncomplaining. The only license John Taylor gave himself, the only hint of sentimentality, was a postscript that appeared on every letter Jacob had received: "If any one of you wants to get a hold of me, I am here for the asking."

In the last letter Jacob had received, John Taylor had said he would be traveling in Africa for six weeks; he would be back sometime in October. So perhaps he was still in Africa.

When Louisa died, Jacob had thought to leave a message on John Taylor's answering machine or write him a note. But he decided against it, decided that his mother wouldn't want John Taylor to know she was dead, wouldn't want him to think for a second that she was no longer in charge of her corner of the world, of her children, wouldn't want him to have the satisfaction of outliving her.

Jacob dialed information for the number of the Urban League in New York, then dialed the number.

Yes, the receptionist said, John Taylor was back from Africa, but he was out of the office for the moment. When she connected Jacob to John Taylor's voice mail, Jacob hung up. Then he dialed Sage's number and left the message that John Taylor was in New York City, working for the Urban League, if she needed to reach him.

Just after he hung up with Sage's answering machine, Caroline phoned.

"Sage called," she said, out of breath, as if she'd been running. "She's being stalked."

"What do you mean, she's being stalked?"

"That's what she said."

"By whom?" Jacob asked. "Did you talk to her?"

"No, I didn't," Caroline said. "But when I got out of the shower, the message was on my machine. She didn't answer when I called back."

"Maybe you should call Security at the university."

"I did," Caroline said. "They told me they've tried her room already and she isn't there. They said there's no evidence of a stalker but they'll check again."

"Tell me exactly what she said."

Caroline turned up the machine so Jacob could hear the message.

"I can't talk now but I had to call you quickly," Sage's voice whispered. "I'm being stalked." And then, as if an afterthought, she added, "By someone I think I know. You've seen him too."

"What do you think?" Caroline asked.

"I think you and Tobias should catch a train for Connecticut, right now," Jacob said. "I'll try to get there too."

Chapter Eleven

Tobias set the cat Faustie down on the bath mat and turned on the hot water in the bathroom. It was dark, as he preferred; what light there was came from the small window by the tub, overlooking an alley where rats meandered slow as caterpillars. He liked candlelight and carried a votive in his pocket, which he lit now and put on the sink, so his face in the mirror seemed haunted and mysterious instead of anemic, as it looked by the harsh light of day.

He wore his curly hair long, as long as it would grow, a beard too, so very little face showed. He looked like Jesus, an agreeable way to look for the moment, allowing him to pass through the world in familiar disguise while he made some decisions.

"Hurry." Caroline was knocking on the door.

He heard her but had no desire to hurry. He wanted to stand under the thin rain of shower water until he felt warm enough to confront what he might have to in Connecticut.

Tobias had been uneasy about Sage for weeks. In her cheerful, industrious phone calls, sometimes three or four a day, she seemed to be shattering from inside out, invisible hairline fractures of the skull.

She was his favorite sister, in fact all of their favorite sister. Placement had something to do with it, the last baby, the black one, the one for whom John Taylor left, or so Mama had always said. The full weight of a broken family. And what kind of legacy was that for a child?

"Not a man to be inconvenienced," was how their mother put it.

"You can't expect rhinestones to turn into diamonds just for the wishing," Aunt Winona said once, cluck-clucking away over one of her thick, floury stews.

"Shut up, Winona," Tobias said. He had shown he was sick of Winona from the time he was old enough to speak in sentences. "This weed's for you, Aunt Winona-pie," he'd say when he was older, lighting up behind her back. "I'm smoking it to suffocate your old Victrola voice screeching in our ears."

But even Aunt Winona, in spite of her gloomy predictions for her niece's future, liked Sage best of all the children. "Lilly Sage is too sweet for the world," she'd say. "Too good."

It wasn't "sweet" or "good" or "smart" or "funny" or any of the other perfectly true descriptions of Sage that mattered to Tobias. It was the fact that she was born with nerves unsheathed, the synapses exposed, the blood too close to the skin, the heart undefended by the rib cage—born colored in a white neighborhood. With the clear eye of an outsider, she saw more than it was good for her to know, more than she could bear.

There were things Tobias noticed in the claustrophobic tent of his own mind, where he spent hours in a half-waking state of examination of his family. He could write books on each of them. He had taken mental notes, memorized exactly. When he lay on Caroline's futon, he was not in a fogged stupor but rather had closed the blinds, turned his attention inward.

As a child, Tobias had been observant, noticing details exactly, able to reproduce them from memory. He had a painter's eye, understood the absent person in a space from the accumulation of details.

"I'm coming," Tobias told Caroline now, but he didn't turn off the shower or step outside its spray.

"I've talked to Jacob," Caroline said. "I'm ready to leave."

Tobias tipped his head back, letting the water spray in his mouth so he couldn't hear Caroline at all. Suddenly she burst through the door and punched her fists at the shower curtain, striking him on one side, enough so he winced in pain.

"I can't stand that you fade out, drowning in your own brain," she said from the other side of the curtain. "We have to hurry."

Tobias pulled the shower curtain back and stepped out naked.

Caroline had picked up Faustie and stood with her arms folded, the cat squished underneath them. "Sage is being stalked," she said furiously.

"Stalked? What do you mean?"

"Just what I said. It's on the answering machine. 'I'm being stalked,' is what she says." Caroline walked out of the bathroom and left the door open. "Please get dressed," she told him.

He walked into the living room, pulling on his blue jeans.

"Don't you ever wear underpants?" she asked.

"I don't think I'll get into that discussion," he said. "The telephone is ringing. You better get it."

Caroline answered. Emmy was calling to say she had found a sitter for Maggie and would be on the next train from Boston. She would wait for Caroline and Tobias in the station.

The train from Thirtieth Street Station headed north over the Schuylkill, and wound around the mustard-yellow art museum. Caroline looked out the window at the city.

"I'm scared," she told Tobias.

"Yeah. I know."

"I wish you could help," Caroline said.

"I will," Tobias said. "I'll help."

He would be solid, he told himself defensively. Solid as a rock, as Mama used to say, hard as steel, tough as nails. That's Tobias Taylor going off to Connecticut, sober as a judge, clean as a whistle, strong as an ox, brave as whatever, on a mission to save his little sister.

"It'll be fine," Tobias said.

"You bet it will." Caroline sank her chin into her jacket collar. "That's just what I was thinking."

Chapter Twelve

This year, I've read a lot about stalkers. They are the subject of the moment in *People* magazine and the tabloids at the drugstore checkout, so it's not hard to come by information.

I've learned stalkers are mostly men, mostly young men like Steven Carney. The ones I've read about don't seem to be bad people with criminal records, not evil or vicious or dangerous by nature. Or even particularly crazy.

What generally happens with a stalker, however, *is* crazy.

A perfectly normal-seeming person meets someone. Maybe he develops a relationship, which goes on and on like those things go. Or maybe not. Either way, something snaps. The electromagnetic field suddenly goes haywire, and he's obsessed.

The first time I looked up the word *obsessed* was in eighth grade, when Aunt Winona made the observation to Emmy who told Caroline who told me that I was developing an obsessive personality.

In my mother's medical encyclopedia, such a person is described as orderly, neat, dependable, but filled with feelings of inadequacy and guilt, open to threat, worry, and indecisiveness. The description fit me perfectly. Just the suggestion made me obsessive, whether or not I had been that way before.

"Don't worry," Mama said. "Every young woman I know with any sensitivity at all meets that description. I did. So did Emmy. So did Caroline."

But I worried. When you're young and in the process of becoming whoever it is you're going to become, you're too susceptible to suggestion.

I made the mistake of mentioning my interest in stalkers to Aunt Winona before I left St. Louis this summer.

"An addictive personality," was her assessment of stalkers. Like alcoholics or drug addicts or over-

eaters. "The solution is substitution," she told me.
"If I had a stalker as a patient, and unfortunately I
never have had, I would recommend the same solution Alcoholics Anonymous requires. Substitution
of one addiction for another. Give yourself over to a
higher power."

As you know, I don't have a lot of confidence in
Winona, but at the moment I'm so desperate I'm
thinking of a substitution for Steven Carney.

"Go have a wine spritzer, Steven," I could say.
"Try a redhead. Or a cigarette."

I mean, it can't be *me* that he's gone on. I've told
you what I look like, black-haired, gray-eyed,
broad-hipped, small pointy breasts. I could go on
and on, and none of it pretty.

So I know I'm Steven Carney's projection of
somebody else, rolled out like dough flat on his
brain, and I've gotten mixed up in the wrong electromagnetic field. If I could just divert his attention;
as it is, he's going to wait outside my door until I
either appear to him or die.

I think of dying.

When I was young, I used to will myself away. In
first grade, Ms. Winer told my mother that I didn't
act like the other girls and seemed to be missing the
equipment necessary at my age to adapt.

Aunt Winona thought Ms. Winer had a point, but my mother told her straight to her face that if she said one more thing about me, in private or in front of the class, she would arrange with some of her black connections to have Ms. Winer sold into slavery.

It worked. I was left alone. But I had to remain in first grade for another seven months after their confrontation, so I learned to will myself away. And then I got good at it.

If things were bad, I'd disappear. In my senior year in high school, I could sit in the front row of assembly invisible. You think you see me—this fast-spreading body, this nappy hair, these doleful gray eyes. But you're wrong. It's me, but there's nobody home. Nothing inside. Gone. Kaput. Zapped by my own desire to be out of this world.

No one knows this about me except Mama. I told her after my sixteenth-birthday party, which Caroline insisted on having, in our backyard with a blues band she knew and all of my high school class. And me, disappearing on the back porch, my absence concealed by the huge smile I slid over my face for the event.

"I used to wear hats," Mama told me when I crawled into bed with her that night. "This was in high school, when I was sure that the eyes of St. Louis were fixed on me. I wanted to hide and thought if I was in a hat, no one would be able to see me."

"Could they see you?" I assumed my mother capable of anything.

"Oh, they could see me just fine. But I didn't know that."

I tried a hat once. It was a maroon beret that I wore dipped over one side of my forehead. I looked very much like a doughnut in a beret—not a look I was hoping to have. I ditched Mama's hat idea and stuck to disappearing without assistance.

"*Sage has* a death wish," Aunt Winona told my mother. She quoted the Romantic poets on the subject of death wishes, and brought the subject up-to-date in the vernacular of the contemporary psychology of her social workers' manual: " 'Death wish' equals 'a wish to die.' "

According to Winona, my death wish is a result of separation anxiety in extremis. "In extremis" is one of Aunt Winona's favorite expressions. The concept of extremism is probably what links Winona to the Romantic poets of the nineteenth century, not a group high on my mother's list of fun reading.

Aunt Winona made an impression. My mother asked me if I had a death wish.

Aunt Winona had that kind of power over her. Let's face it, she was the older sister, and like a lot of people who lack imagination, she lives by information she memorizes from books or newspapers, which gives her a straight shot at power, without diversions.

"I don't have a death wish," I told my mother. "I have a wish to metamorphose."

That was it, of course. To change into a wholly different form. A butterfly is what I had in mind. The stage of development I'm now in—the stage I prefer—is that of cocoon.

So it's not a death wish, exactly, that preoccupies me, but rather a wish to remain in the mummified disguise of a cocoon, in a room from which I can see everything around me clearly but in which no one can see me while I wait on the butterfly.

There are eight messages on my machine, and the clock has stopped. It must be noon, the sounds outside tell me; veiled sun spreads smoky light over the room, there is bustle in the corridor.

I keep the answering machine turned down, so I don't have to hear the messages as the calls come in. I know that one is from Emmy, one or maybe two are from Jacob, and one is from the professor of my chemistry lab. Tobias never calls. He doesn't need to. We are always in touch.

Since Steven Carney returned from breakfast, something is changing. The atmosphere in the room has thinned. Perhaps I have been breathing my own air for too long.

In high school biology we learned that when a person is dying—not a quick, unexpected dying but a slow shutting down—the balance of oxygen and carbon dioxide shifts and the body is slowly poisoned by an accumulation of carbon dioxide.

I feel lightheaded, disassociated, as if I were an abstraction of myself in which my skeleton has been adjusted and the right and left sides of my body no longer fit together.

I feel as if I were slipping out of the world.

In times of trouble like this, I try to phone my father. I search for him thoughtfully, ten numbers at a time, checking off one after another with a notation if there is any possibility. Today I move to Cleveland. I got xeroxed copies of the John Taylor entries from phone books at the library. There are several John Taylors in Cleveland, and even a John Jefferson Taylor; I'll call him first.

"Hello," I say. "I'm calling for John Jefferson Taylor."

The woman who has answered the phone is elderly and slow to respond, so I ask her again.

"Jefferson is in the hospital, as you very well know," she says.

"Actually, I didn't know that," I tell her. "I'm a stranger."

"Well, you shouldn't be phoning here if you're a

stranger," she says, although her tone doesn't have the sharpness of her words.

"I'm sorry." I go on to tell her my name and my situation. "I've lost my father," I say, surprised at myself, because I'm not confessional by nature. "And so I'm spending time telephoning people who have his name."

"He lives in Cleveland?" the woman asks.

"I don't know where he lives."

"Well, I'm in Cleveland. Did you know you were calling Cleveland?"

"I know," I say, and thank her and hang up.

C*old*, not even cold specifically but cooling down, my body heat descending, I crawl under the bed, pulling a comforter over me, although I know in my rational mind that my room is hot.

I don't have the energy to try another John Taylor, or even to write on my Fear List the new fear rising over my bed in a tidal wave.

11. Dying

Chapter Thirteen

I took all of the pictures of Mama and me from St. Louis.

I tend to be diffident, as you can tell. I'm in the habit of saying "You go first" or "Never mind" or "That's fine, anything you want." I don't put myself forward.

But going through the boxes of photographs in the back room of our house on Moran Street, the morning before I left to return to Martha's Vineyard and pack up for college, I said I wanted all of the pictures of Mama and me.

"All?" Caroline asked, holding a photograph of me when I was maybe six months old, with a mass of curls, lying on Mama's bed with her, pulling her long red hair.

"All," I answered.

"Let Sage have them," Emmy said.

My family is careful with me.

I don't look at the pictures of Mama and me. I haven't since I arrived at this university. I can't. But there is one I'm searching for now, because in it Mama has such a lovely expression, such generosity as she looks at me, that I have to believe in my heart she's very glad that when the choice came to keep me or not, she made the choice she did.

In the photograph, it's my third birthday and I'm wearing a bright pink pointed party hat and holding an unhappy kitten. The kitten, whom I called Betty Boo, was my present from Aunt Winona. Shortly after my third birthday, Boo chose to move in with Winona—and she still lives with her, peeing in Winona's closet and not mine. As is clear from this photograph, I was not the owner Boo hoped to have.

Mama is kneeling beside me, her head upturned so her long hair falls away from her face. She is smiling. Around us, not in the picture but surely there, are my brothers and sisters and Winona, who was taking the picture.

What I love about this picture is the familiar sense it gives me of my childhood, especially now. I *know* this picture in my bones.

"Smile," Winona is saying. "Look here, Lilly.
Smile at Aunt Winona."
I am scowling, looking at the ground.
"Look at Aunt Winona and smile," Tobias imitates.
"Careful of the kitty," Emmy is calling. "Careful
of the kitty or you'll kill her, Lilly."
I squeeze the kitten tight in my small arms and
bury my face in her fur.
"Is she squeezing the kitten too hard, Louisa?"
Winona puts down the camera and rushes over to
check on Boo.
"If the kitten dies, Mama will resuscitate her," Ja-
cob says calmly. "That's why she's a doctor."
"She's not a kitten doctor, stupid," Caroline says.
"She's a human doctor."
Betty Boo is squealing, scrambling frantically to
get out of my grip. Mama gently tries to pry my arms
open, kissing me lightly on the cheek, whispering a
story in my ear to distract me.
"Just let me check, Lilly," she is saying to me.
"Boo may be having appendicitis."
"She doesn't have appendicitis," Tobias says.
"She's being squeezed to death."
And he runs around the backyard screaming
cheerfully that Boo Boo Boo is squished, squashed,
squooshed.
Winona is crying.

I haven't mentioned that Winona is a person of
homogenized sensibilities. Sentimentality is the

highest emotion she aspires to, and that, according to Mama, is a sign of meanness. Winona is mean. I can say that even though we are related; fortunately my blood has been thickened by slavery a few times removed.

Mama releases Boo from my arms; this breaks my heart. I fall on my stomach and scream. Emmy takes the kitten and hands her to a weeping Winona, and Jacob picks me up off the ground and hands me to Mama.
"Here's your precious baby girl," he says. "Your million-dollar baby."
"My precious baby girl," Mama says, kissing me from head to toe. "My sweet angel."
And I float into her arms, slide through her skin, into her bloodstream, safe.

We occasionally have serious family talks. In fact, we always have them when we're together, and they're intended to be a kind of self-promotion. Family promotion, more accurately.

Early in our lives, we didn't know any other children of what's now called a biracial marriage. Not until later did we meet any. And so we lived in a single-parent family, passing as white, with a living father who was not permitted through the front door.

Which is where the self-promotion comes in.

We had no place to set our feet except on Mama's soil, and that was only half our story. So we invented one, sanctifying our own mythology with a kind of cultural pride, as if we were members of a large and important tribe instead of the motley band of five children growing up in a world we probably conceived as hostile.

The last family discussions we had were in September, when everyone met at Woods Hole to take me to college, and stayed at a Holiday Inn along the way, where we all slept in the same room and ordered in Chinese food.

That night we talked about how you know things. For instance, I *know* that birthday party photographed by Winona, even though I don't remember details or how Mama looked then. I have only scraps of memory that don't really fit together to constitute a story. So I make the story up.

"If you don't remember it, it isn't true," Jacob said.

"Yes it is," Emmy answered. "We can't know everything. I guess at Mama's life with John Taylor from letters and pictures and what she said and what I want to believe."

"It's real because you think it is," Tobias said, defining his own brand of stoned reality.

"Besides," Caroline said. "We can't exactly have an objective reporter covering our personal story. We have to guess at some things."

"We have Winona," I said, and everybody laughed.

Now and then in the days, maybe even weeks, I've been hidden away from Steven Carney in room A426—how long has it been now? I'm losing track, the days fall together like the long shadows of trees, and it's difficult to know where one ends and another begins—now and then I have thought about *knowing*, about putting together my life as if a personal history were simply a hint, a collection of dots on a page, and my job were to connect them.

I am still under the bed, trapped here in permanent discomfort, and it seems to be getting dark. There's only a long rectangle of light that slides behind the bed where I'm lying, and either the sun has moved out of reach of my windows or else it's turned gray and rainy outside. Perhaps the steady sound I hear is in my head.

I daydream of calling Mama.

"Hello, Mama," I say.

"Hello, Sage," she says to me, confirming my existence. "Hello. Hello."

Chapter Fourteen

The telephone in my room is ringing as usual, probably the dean or my organic chemistry professor or Emmy or Caroline. But now I hear that it's Jacob: there he is on my answering machine.

I pull the covers off my head so I can hear him.

"Sagie, it's Jacob," he says, as if I couldn't recognize his voice. "If you need to call John Taylor, he's in New York City, working for the Urban League. Sage?"

But the phone clicks off, and I pull the covers back over my head. Shaking, my heart drumbeating in my mouth, my stomach overturned, I press my pillow against my ears.

The letters from John Taylor that we didn't divide up were boxed, to go to Emmy's, in case the house does sell. Winona has decided to sell her half of the duplex too; she and Boo will move into an apartment above her office so she can be a full-service twenty-four-hour social worker.

I have been over and over the letters I have. A few days ago, though, I found an envelope at the bottom of the shoe box that I had not seen before, with five letters in it.

The first is dated May 2, 1980. I was almost two years old. There must have been a check in this one, because John Taylor mentions it. But the check is gone, of course, and there's a line in red marker drawn diagonally across the letter—Mama's work.

> Louisa, I've been thinking how crazy it is going on like this. I want to see my children. Our children. This doesn't make sense. I don't know very much about forgiveness, but for a Christian,

you've got an attitude. Or are you a Christian?
Maybe that's the trouble. This month I'm send-
ing an extra $200. *Splurge.* JJT

The second letter I found is dated October 11,
1986, and written on yellow legal paper. It's hard to
read because the pen was running out of ink:

L—sometimes I think about Venus and it makes
me sick. Things started to fall out with us when
she died. Who did we think we were—trying to
save the world—a colored man and his optimistic
wife. JJT

The third is typewritten on business stationery.
It's not dated, but I have a feeling it's an early letter, written two or three years after John Taylor
left.

Dear Louisa, I have taken a job as a field director
with the Urban League in Chicago, working primarily with project children. I'm pleased with
the work. It's not entirely hopeless.

I live alone in an apartment in Lincolnwood.
Mostly I work, although I have taken up the pi-
ano, which gives me a lot of happiness and I'm
not bad at it. I play clubs.

I do not have a girlfriend and would never

consider having another child. I'm surprised you asked.

Is there any chance you could come to Chicago for a weekend? I know you're extremely busy but I'd like to see you. I won't make it difficult. You call the shots. Yrs. John

Mama must have written him before this letter and then, after the invitation to Chicago, never written him back. That is my guess.

He waited too long to ask for her. Maybe her head could have turned before she finished medical school, but by the time she was a physician, she no longer believed in miracles. She was a stubborn woman.

The letter dated October 15, 1988, is a sheet of paper with just a couple of lines:

I'd be grateful if you'd send me a picture of our children. JJT

The most recent letter is written on the back of a laundry list and dated December 23, 1993. John Taylor doesn't mention Christmas.

Louisa, I'm moving to NYC, to work for the Urban League. I understand from a personal contact who sent me a picture that the baby turned out

smart. In the picture, she looks nice like my Aunt
Beatrice, who used to take me to the movies
when I was young. John

I have that letter in a picture frame. Not so the
words show and people can read them, but to keep
it safe.

Chapter Fifteen

Emmy arrived at the station first and waited for the train from Philadelphia, which was a half-hour late. She called Sage's room and then the dean. She was in a meeting, but her secretary knew all about Sage Taylor and said she was glad the family had come.

"Do you know something you're not telling me?" Emmy asked.

"I'm only a secretary here. I can't say anything more."

"Why not? Why can't you tell me if something worse has happened?"

"Nothing worse has happened that I know of," the secretary said.

"Do you know about the stalker?" Emmy asked. "Did the dean mention that to you?"

"The stalker?"

The stalker who's outside my sister's room, stupid, Emmy thought.

"Oh, yes," the secretary said, as if the stalker was the subject of a private joke. "Security checked. There was no evidence of a stalker, as far as I know."

Jacob's answering machine was on when Emmy called him. The recording was curt. His number, and "Please leave a message."

She crossed her fingers, hoping against hope that Jacob had decided to catch a plane.

When their Amtrak train finally arrived, twenty minutes later, Caroline got out first. White-faced and shaken, she held on to Tobias's arm. Emmy was waiting for them.

"Do you think Jacob is coming?" Caroline asked. "I need him to come."

"I don't know," Emmy said. "I called and the machine was on."

"I can take care of everything," Tobias said. "Depend on me."

"We do," Emmy said sweetly. "I promise we do."

"I'll try," Caroline said. "But it's a little like learning a foreign language."

Emmy took their arms. "We have to stick together," she said.

The taxi dropped them off in front of Emerson Hall. It was just after five o'clock, the sun dipping behind the large stone building where Sage lived, the sidewalks bustling with students.

"What are we going to do?" Caroline asked. "This is making me sick."

They walked to the entrance of Emerson Hall under a long shadow of trees, over the blanket of crisp yellow leaves, the familiar smell of autumn around them, and the noisy cries of birds headed south.

"I have an intuition," Emmy said.

"Don't tell me," Caroline said.

"No, it's a good intuition."

"You think she's alive?" Caroline asked.

"Of course she's alive," Tobias said. "I know that. Emmy knows it."

"Do you promise?" Caroline asked. "Otherwise I don't think I can go in here."

"I promise," Tobias said. "Count on me. I absolutely promise."

A boy in blue sweats let them in the front door. "We're here to see our sister," Emmy said. "Sage Taylor."

"Sage Taylor? Isn't she the one in A426?"

"Yes," Emmy said. "That's her room number."

The boy gave them a peculiar look. "There's a crowd up there."

"And is Sage there?" Emmy asked.

He shrugged. "I don't know anything." He pointed to the elevator.

"I want to walk," Caroline said. "I never go on elevators."

"We can walk," Tobias said.

But Caroline got on the elevator anyway. Emmy punched the button, and when the doors opened on the fourth floor, the crowd was assembled just ahead of them—a group of six or seven people.

Jacob was there, standing next to a small man in a dark suit, his back to the elevator.

"It's Jacob," Emmy said. "Look ahead of us."

"It *is* Jacob," Caroline said.

The man standing next to Jacob turned in their direction.

Caroline held on to her sister's hand and Tobias's, and took a huge breath to keep from fainting. "Oh my God," she said. "Oh my good God."

The man walked with Jacob down the corridor toward them. His hair was cut short as a tight cap around his head; his fine, sharp-featured face was known in the marrow to them all.

"It *is* John Taylor, isn't it, Em?" Caroline whispered. "Isn't it?"

But Emmy didn't answer. She couldn't answer. And when Caroline looked over at her for confirmation, Emmy was weeping.

"Yes," Tobias said, grabbing his sisters. "Yes. Yes. Yes."

Chapter Sixteen

The summer before my senior year in high school, before my mother died, it was just Mama and me. I should have known something was the matter with her heart, because the oxygen wasn't getting to her blue eyes. The irises looked sometimes glassy, sometimes dead. And her hands shook enough to call attention to themselves.

That summer I cooked dinner, homemade rosemary bread and fresh tomatoes, white beans and tuna, vegetable chili with hot peppers. I'd come

home from work at Piggly Wiggly, where I un-
packed boxes, after stopping by Fresh Market for
groceries. Sometimes Jacob would be at home, but
mostly it was me and Mama, and Winona on the
telephone from San Francisco, where she was
spending the summer studying addictions. I'd put
candles on the table in the dining room, and sweet-
smelling phlox from our garden, and then, just as
we started supper, Winona would call.

Mama always talked to her, although her part of
the exchange was silence or "No, Winona" or
"Please" or "I'm too exhausted for addictions tonight." She'd hang up, rest her chin in one hand,
and try to eat. I noticed that she didn't swallow.
She pushed her food into a corner of the plate, pil-
ing it high so she seemed to be eating, or spread the
food around the edges so it seemed to disappear.

She didn't eat and she didn't sleep.

I'd hear her walking back and forth from the
kitchen to the living room to the study downstairs,
all night long. I didn't sleep either. I sat on my bed
or on the top step upstairs and listened to her agi-
tated meanderings.

Of course she couldn't sleep, she was too hungry.
She never ate.

"I'm not hungry," she said. "I eat a lot."

I didn't argue.

I did eat. I ate my dinner and hers and leftovers.
That's the summer I began to expand to the width

of my present form, which spills over the sides of this dormitory bed.

One August night, hot, too hot for St. Louis, the air-conditioning out on the second floor of our house, I lay on the couch downstairs in darkness and watched Mama in a long white gown, her hair in a loose braid down her back, standing in the study going through the pictures of our childhood.

It was odd to see her looking through photographs. She was not a woman to be taken with the past. Unsentimental, her eye was on tomorrow.

She called out, "Lilly," knowing I wasn't sleeping. I can keep no secrets from her. When she called me, I had been imagining her young.

From a distance, she looked like a girl, especially with her braid. She was something when she was young—tall and reedy, with a mass of dark red hair against her pale, fawn-spotted skin, her eyes, by contrast, bluer than they were now. Not much older than I am when she met John Taylor. Maybe nineteen. Pregnant with Emmy when they were married by a justice of the peace at the Arkansas–Missouri border, on their way to meet my mother's disapproving parents in St. Louis.

This news, the negative details, I have from Aunt Winona.

The love story is from Emmy.

"Lilly," Mama called again. "Look here."

Just at the moment I was thinking of her as a girl,

she was looking at a picture of herself at nineteen. We had an invisible silk cord between us, Mama and I. She had heard my thoughts, the sound inaudible, the waves registering on her brain.

Sometimes it is unbearable to imagine your mother young.

The picture was front on. She was wearing blue jean overalls without a shirt, her pudding-soft breasts spreading just outside the bib. Her hair was long and frizzy, and her hands were folded under her belly. Her smile, so pleased, so smug and cat-like, made her face luminous.

I looked at the picture under the lamp.

"You were amazing," I told her.

"I was pregnant. I was nineteen years old that summer, just nineteen." She laughed. "And I thought I knew everything."

"You seem to be very happy," I said.

"I was. Of course I was."

She sank into a chair, drew her knees up under her chin and looked at me. Not an expression I recognized. Wistful, almost fragile.

"I have never talked to you about romance," she said.

"Romance" is my mother's word for sex. Not that she's used it with me, but Caroline and Emmy told me how sweet they thought it was that she had an old-fashioned word for sex.

Winona, whose experience with romance is in

the debit column, calls it "sex," making the *x* sound of death.

"No," I told Mama, "you haven't told me about romance."

She was beautiful in the soft dim light of her study. By day, she was more red-haired Irish than Swede, and familiar-looking in the Catholic Midwest, except for her height. But my father, a small wiry black man with attitude—that's Jacob's description of him—must have found her exotic. He must have seen a perfect loveliness, a watercolor face, liquid pale blue eyes, soft wavy feather-pillow hair.

"I had other boyfriends before I met your father," she said. There was a girlishness about her, the way she turned her head at an angle, put her chin over her knees. "But no romance," she said, lacing her fingers. "Your father was like tornado weather."

I sat very still, expecting some details, but she had nothing more to report.

"You can have the picture if you like," she finally said.

She gave me three other pictures that night. They were all of me: at three with Caroline, on my fourth birthday alone, and one I didn't recall seeing before. In this picture I am on my back, a plump naked chocolate-brown baby with a mop of curly black hair, my fat legs kicking, my expression sour.

"That may be the earliest picture of you, Lilly,"
Mama said. "I was so harried that year I didn't get
around to pictures." She held it up to the light.
"You looked a little like Emmy when you were a
baby."

The baby was unfamiliar. Not like the other Taylor babies I'd seen in pictures. Broader, browner,
cheerless.

"Emmy is white in her baby pictures," I said
combatively. "She looks white now."

Mama looked up startled. "No," she said. "Not
really."

We almost never talked about race. We had been
taught by Mama that we were blessed to be true
Americans—black and white, Irish and African and
Scandinavian and Creole, with a little of Eastern
Europe from her grandmother Rachel.

But the subject stopped short of race.

I knew in my heart that we were white as far as
Mama was concerned: her babies, earned, fought
for, won—and therefore as white as she was, white
as the corner of St. Louis where I had grown up,
my birthright, where I belonged.

"Emmy looks white and I look black," I said,
"don't you think?"

"I don't think about it," Mama answered.

"I do. Because of Winona."

"What has Winona said to you?"

"Winona told me that John Taylor asked you to
get rid of me."

"She told you that?"

"She said you refused to have an abortion."

Mama crossed her legs and folded her arms in a serious manner.

"So when you wouldn't have an abortion, John Taylor left," I continued. "That's what Winona said."

"You shouldn't believe everything you hear, Lilly."

"What should I believe, then?" I was braver with my mother than usual because lately she seemed different, capable of weakness.

"You should believe what I told you tonight," she replied. "About romance."

I am awake in my room, dreaming of tornado weather.

We have tornados in Missouri, particularly across the land above the Ozarks where my grandparents have a farm and where we used to go summers when I was younger, when we were all children.

These visits were our summer vacation, and they went on for a month while Mama stayed in St. Louis working. The idea that it was a vacation ruined the concept of holidays for me for good.

The farm would have been more agreeable with animals, but there were none, not even a cat. My grandparents, and especially my tightlipped grandmother, were severe, silent people without a capacity for affection. The food was bad. The only cheerful memory I have of those summers was the time we spent in the hot attic above the kitchen. I went with Emmy and Caroline, and they smoked and talked about sex. Particularly sex between our grandparents.

"It's amazing how they got Winona and Mama," Emmy said once.

"Not by anything they did together, for sure." Caroline giggled.

"So what did they do?" Emmy asked. "Him on the bottom, or her?"

"Neither," Caroline said. "Him in the bathroom with the door locked and his pants hanging down around his ankles."

"And he has a little sterilized jar, right?" Emmy asked.

"Exactly," Caroline said. "And he puts the little wigglies in the jar."

"Where does he get the little wigglies?" I didn't participate in these sexual discussions unless I was completely in the dark. And then I asked a question, and the question always pleased my sisters to death.

"So Grandpa has a penis, right, Lil?" Caroline asked.

"I guess," I said.

"Count on it for peeing," Emmy said.

"And he takes hold of his penis," Caroline demonstrated with an invisible penis coming out of her belly. "He rubs it up and down and up and down, and bonanza—out come the little wigglies into the sterilized jar."

"Little wigglies?" I asked.

"Sperm," Emmy said. "Permed sperm. Remember I told you sperm plus egg equals baby?"

"I remember," I said.

"So then he puts a top on the jar," Caroline went on, "and puts the jar in a brown paper lunch bag, puts the bag in the refrigerator, and Grandma takes it out, goes into the bathroom, locks the door, and pours the jar of wigglies in."

"Bonanza!" Emmy laughed so hard she couldn't sit up. "Winona."

The only other pleasure I can remember was tornados.

Tornado weather is like nothing I have ever known. Suddenly, as if an engine turned off or God pushed a button and the earth quit—*whoom*, the world goes still. Hot-death still. Not a movement, not a sound in the air. And you *know*. You feel blue danger at the center of your being, your mouth is bone-dry.

The tornado is moving in your direction. You see it twisting off in the distance, a giant slate-gray top gyrating through the sky, the sky blackening, and then the roar.

Lie facedown on the ground, arms splayed. If you're close enough to shelter, go to the middle of the house, to the cellar if there is one. Those are the rules for tornados.

My grandparents' farm has never taken a direct hit.

But I know the sudden silence, the thrilling fragility in my groin. And then the inky darkness, a wild charge across the flat land toward me, where I am standing—will I die here?—a small, lone girl aching for excitement.

I see my grandmother on the front porch.

"Come in, Lilly," she is calling. "Hurry. We can't tell the direction the storm might take."

"Come straight in this house, Lilly Taylor," my grandfather shouts in his hard frozen voice.

But I am not listening to their warnings of tornado weather.

"*Sage?*" is the call from the other side of my door. "Sage."

I want to say, "Yes."

"Yes, come in, Steven Carney. Push down the door, rush in my direction. I'm here waiting for you."

"Sage Taylor, open the door."

I'm shivering, though it's very warm. I know it's

warm. I pull the down comforter over my face and listen to the banging on my door.

"Open the door," he is shouting.

The corridors must be empty, or he wouldn't call attention to himself like this. There is only the poor manic-depressive locked in his own room down the hall, under the covers as I am, wishing for death.

Chapter Seventeen

Steven Carney is here, but I can't see him. He has broken through the door and is calling my name. I can hear him clearly. He's calling, "Sage, Sage," and I hear him from the tunnel into which I seem to have fallen. At least it sounds like a tunnel: hollow, reverberating, plaintive, the way tunnel sound is captured like a blue note forced through a trumpet.

But I can't see him.

I can't see at all.

I seem to have lost my sight, as if I'd had a blow to the head, although I don't remember the blow and I feel no bump when I put my hand on the crown.

But the sense I have, the foggy and confusing sense of where I am and what is going on, suggests a concussion.

He's in the room. I can smell him, the heavy, musty smell of a man bearing down on me. I'm not able to protest.

I seem to have lost my voice. I hear the words I'm trying to say in my head, but they aren't projected beyond me into the room so I can make myself understood, so I can protest.

I feel as if he had pulled off the comforter under which I've been hiding. The autumn weather—a windy day with a hint of winter—is blowing across, chilling me. I'm bare-skinned. He's taken off my black pants, my lacy underwear—Caroline insisted on lace—his hands are under my shirt, on my breasts. My breasts are expanding, filling his large hands with the water weight of late-summer peaches.

I have lost a sense of reality, a sense of where I begin and where I end, of whether Steven Carney is in this room with me as I imagine him to be, or not.

I'm very small. Only the size of an ordinary pencil, a beech twig, the stem of a tall crimson dahlia, the size of a child. But he's found me and I feel the weight of him, a large, hard-skinned man, naked.

"Rape!" I scream.

Can anyone hear me? Is that a sound I've made?

"Rape! I'm being raped."

Is there anybody here, anybody in this building but the manic-depressive sleeping in room A417?

I struggle out of bed, lightheaded, teetering. I know I'm teetering. He must be somewhere, but since my sight has gone, I've lost my equilibrium. I can feel him in a corner of my room, where I must have thrown him when I struggled underneath the violent weight of his body.

"Rape!" I call, pushing the dresser away from the door, where he must have put it to conduct this violation in private.

I have the strength of an animal.

The dresser moves. I break open the door to my room, which he has locked against invasion, and to my surprise, there's a crowd in the corridor. I can't see them but I sense their presence, and I promise myself I'll speak calmly and tell the truth. They must take me seriously.

"I have been raped." I think I hear my voice tumbling forward into the group of listeners. "A man called Steven Carney has been stalking me and is in my bedroom now, crouching in the corner."

I hope I'm right. I assume he's there. He's somewhere, but I can't see, and now this thinness in my brain is taking over. I'm going to faint.

"Sage." It sounds like Emmy's voice. It must be Emmy. I believe I've fallen on the floor. I don't have a real sense of my body and where it's placed. This is perhaps the feeling of a person who's been beheaded—the body is separated from the head, but for a brief moment the person hasn't entirely lost the capacity to think.

"She's so thin." The voice is Caroline's. "Emaciated. Oh, Sagie, you mustn't have eaten for days."

"Weeks." Someone I don't recognize is speaking, a deep-voiced woman with a cold. "We believe she's been in her room for weeks. Two at least. Maybe even three."

I want to protest, but I've swallowed my voice. I want to tell them I've been here only since the arrival of Steven Carney on this miserable campus.

"Jesus, Sage. You poor chicken." I hear Tobias. He's very close to me, right beside me. I smell cinnamon on his breath. "Sagie, can you hear me?"

I say, "Yes, of course," but no one appears to have heard.

"Is she conscious?" Tobias asks.

Of course I'm conscious, I want to say, but I don't bother, since evidently my voice is gone.

Someone else besides Tobias is close by, I think a woman. I hope it's not Daphne; I'm not in a state of mind to make sexual decisions. The woman's cold hands are resting on my head, pleasant and reassuring.

"I don't believe she's conscious," the woman is saying. "I think she's been without food and water for too long. She's lost consciousness from dehydration."

"Can she hear me?" Tobias asks.

"No, she can't," the cool-handed woman says.

People are peculiar in what they think they know about other people—Winona, for instance, knowing so much and understanding nothing.

"Will she die?" It's Caroline, reasonable, sensible Caroline, falling apart.

"Her vital signs are weak," the woman says. "Her pulse is slow, her blood pressure very low."

"An ambulance is coming," someone says.

"Will she die?" Caroline asks again. "Please, someone tell me."

"No, she won't die." It's a voice I haven't heard before, a man's deep rolling voice. I'm happy he is here to reassure my family, since I am unable to do so.

"Sage," Tobias says in my ear. "Can you hear me?"

"I'm listening," I say.

"Please. I want to tell you something. I want you to hear me."

I turn my face toward him.

"I think she can hear me," he says. "Do you see? She's turned her face." He leans very close. I can feel his lips against my cheek.

"John Taylor is here."

"John Taylor is here?" I ask. "Here where I am? My father is here?"

"Pick her up," someone says.

I think it's Emmy, but she is far away.

"May I pick her up?"

It's the voice of the man who spoke earlier and promised my family I wouldn't die.

"You can pick her up," the woman with cool hands says.

He's putting his arms around me and I'm trembling against his warm body, the blood beginning to unfreeze in my veins, lifted off the ground, into the air, light as dust, contained in the arms of a man who smells of pine.

Someone says the ambulance has arrived; I haven't heard any sirens. My father is telling me that I'm going to the hospital to be examined, that my family will be with me there.

"Can you hear me?" he asks.

"I can hear you," I answer.

"I doubt she can," the cool-handed woman says.

"Never mind," my father says. "I'll talk to her anyway. Who knows what she can hear?"

"I'm sorry this has happened," a familiar voice is saying, probably the dean's. "I wish we had known there was family trouble."

"There wasn't family trouble," Caroline says crossly. "Sage was being stalked."

"We checked thoroughly. There's no evidence

whatsoever that she was being stalked," the dean says. "I think it's more likely that she has been hallucinating because of starvation and dehydration."

Caroline says something I don't hear, and Tobias tells her to hush, to get in the ambulance pronto and hush.

There's an argument about who will go in the ambulance. A man's authoritative voice says only one person can go.

"We're all going," my father says.

"A rule is a rule," the man says.

But my father, his voice extremely calm, says no. Everyone in the family must go with me in the ambulance to the hospital.

We are inside. I sense the dimensions of the van and I'm lying now on a stretcher, amid the scrambling, high-spirited talk of my family.

"It's difficult to believe you're here," Caroline says when we begin to move.

"I can't believe it either," Emmy says.

I haven't heard Jacob's voice yet, but I hear him now. He must have come all the way from St. Louis to be here.

"Do you know about Mama?" Caroline is asking.

"Jacob told me." John Taylor has a lovely low, cozy voice, unlike any of the voices I heard on the telephone in the time I've been looking for him. "It broke my heart," he says.

There is a long silence, I think it's long. I have no

sense of time, no sense of its passing or standing still. I must be sleeping off and on, but I hear everything around me.

Tobias is weeping.

"Who called you?" Emmy is asking.

"Sage did," John Taylor replies.

"Sage?" Emmy says. "Sage called you?"

"She left a message on my voice mail at the office."

"How did she find you?" Caroline's voice is hard.

"I don't know," John Taylor says. "She just left a message."

"And she told you to come here?" Tobias asks.

"She said she was being stalked. She asked me to come."

"I knew where our father was," Jacob says quietly.

"How did you know?" Caroline asks. "How come we didn't all know?"

"Because of Mama. I've known because I wrote him letters. I've told him about us."

"I'm amazed," Emmy says in a faraway tone I haven't heard before. "I can't believe this has happened."

"You've been here all along," Caroline says. "And you've never been in touch."

"I've thought about you," John Taylor says.

"Then you should have called us," Caroline says.

"Was Mama fierce enough to keep you from coming?" Emmy asks.

"She could be fierce. And when she made up her mind . . ." John Taylor says this as if merely the suggestion of Mama's stubbornness is sufficient.

He's leaning over me now. I can feel his breath close to my face. I hope I don't look too awful, too fat or broken out.

My hair is dirty.

"Sage is going to be okay," Emmy says. "I have an instinct." Maybe it is her hand I feel on my wrist.

"I know she will be," my father says.

The ambulance moves in fits and starts. I don't hear the sound of the siren, but it must be blaring, or maybe my situation is not an emergency. It doesn't feel like an emergency. The air in here is warm, and the voices of my family wash over me like summer sun.

I turn in the direction of my father.

"Do you see?" he says. "Sage is looking at me."

Soon, when I am examined by the doctors at the hospital and released, I will thank my father for coming.

I hope he will be able to hear me.

Chapter Eighteen

At the hospital, Tobias found himself in charge, moving between the dark room where Sage lay too still and the brightly lit waiting room where his family sat with the families of others.

"You stay with her," Jacob had told Tobias. "If she wakes up, she might talk to you."

And Tobias did, standing at the bottom of the bed or sitting in a chair beside her, holding Sage's hand, leaning over her, while the others came in and out.

The first night Sage almost died. By the time the ambulance reached the hospital, she had fallen into a deep coma and the doctors couldn't stabilize her blood pressure.

"I don't know," the physician in charge said. "It doesn't look good."

"You have to do something," Caroline pleaded.

"He is," Jacob said. "They're doing their best."

*M*ost of the first day, the family sat in the waiting room, wary with John Taylor but gentle with one another, their eyes fixed on the door as they awaited the doctors' report.

"Has she moved yet?" they asked Tobias when he joined them.

"Not yet. But she will."

"Don't kid yourself," Caroline said crossly.

Tobias shrugged. He wasn't going to argue with Caroline, but he believed Sage was going to live.

Early on the morning of the second day, the waiting room full of the family of an accident victim, Caroline exploded at her father. She rose from the couch where she was sitting, and picked up a side table and threw it at him, scattering magazines and bottles of soda, and splintering the table against the floor.

After that incident, the head nurse arranged for the family to have a private waiting room near Sage's room and away from the main waiting room. After all, she said, the family needed to be together and not with strangers.

But Caroline was the real reason, and anyone could see that she was likely to lose her temper again.

Later she told Tobias that she had been sitting quietly watching John Taylor and the temper came up suddenly like sickness. She couldn't control herself. "I don't know what came over me. I am so furious at him for being here, for coming into our lives at the last moment."

The private room was small, with a view of a parking lot below and offices on the other wing. The television set in it was never on. For most of the three days, the family kept the door shut and sat pressed together in very little comfort, trying to make sense of John Taylor's long absence, of Sage's disintegration.

Except Caroline, who stood alone next to the window, her arms folded tightly across her chest, a fixed expression on her face.

"What happened with our parents happened," Tobias told her once when John Taylor was gone from the room. "We can never understand why."

"So I'm supposed to forgive him for not coming back?" Caroline asked. "Fat chance."

"Maybe he couldn't," Jacob said. "Think of it that way."

"There are telephones and telegraphs and trains and airplanes." Caroline put her head in her hands. "He could have come back, and he didn't."

But over the three long days and nights, trapped in the waiting room, Tobias could tell that his brother and sisters were gradually accommodating their father.

They watched John Taylor when he wasn't looking. They took the whole of him into account, softening to the familiarity of his presence in their lives, the desolation in his dark eyes, the sense of him in a room.

He was their father.

He did not apologize or accuse Louisa or excuse himself.

As he sat in the straight-back chair and stared out of the window into the gray autumn day, they began to understand that John Taylor had loved their mother. They felt his sadness; even in her absence, she had captured a part of him that was inviolate.

"I like him," Emmy said once, with John Taylor out of the room.

"I think he's a good man," Jacob said. "It can't have been easy."

"I had no idea I was from this family of turn-the-other-cheek wimps," Caroline said. "Especially you, Tobias. I thought you hated him too. That's what you said lying around my studio in a druggy cloud."

"I love him," Tobias answered. "I used to think that if I ever saw him, he'd be a stranger, and he isn't."

Tobias was standing at the foot of her bed when Sage regained consciousness. She looked at him and her eyes held, but she didn't speak.

"She's going to be okay," the doctor said.

"She can't talk," Emmy insisted. She and Tobias followed the doctor out of the room.

"She doesn't want to talk yet," Tobias said.

"She isn't ready," the doctor agreed. She hadn't eaten for three weeks, he reminded them. She had drunk very little water. She had begun to hallucinate from dehydration and finally had lost consciousness. "Her body very nearly shut down for good."

"What about her mind?" Caroline asked.

"I don't know about her mind. My job is the body."

"She's not crazy, if that's what you're asking, Caroline," Tobias said. "We'll know soon enough what happened to her, because she'll tell us."

"How do you know?" Caroline asked. "She hasn't been telling us the truth lately."

"I just know."

Sage spoke to Tobias first. He was sitting beside her, playing with her fingers, telling her about the time in second grade when Mickey Englefield had lifted her yellow sundress and smelled the skirt and how Tobias had tried to push Mickey over and missed, when she turned her head toward him.

"Do you think I was raped?" she asked.

"No, I don't think so," Tobias answered.

"I thought I was being raped by Steven Carney. I thought he finally broke into my room."

"That didn't happen," Tobias said.

"Did you hear me shouting 'Rape'?"

"You were unconscious when we saw you. You didn't say anything that we could hear."

"And Steven Carney wasn't there?"

"Maybe he was there somewhere, but no one found him," Tobias said gently. "No one on your hall remembers any stranger. Are you sure it was him?"

"Maybe I thought he was there," Sage said. "Maybe."

"And he wasn't really."

"That could have happened."

"It's weird, isn't it? I even sort of wanted him to be there. Do you think it's weird, Tobias?"

"Not that weird. You were very lonely, and you didn't want to bother your family about loneliness."

"I guess," Sage said.

"You could have called me, you know."

"I know."

Tobias sat down on her bed and leaned back against her pillow, his bony shoulder pressed into hers.

"Do you like John Taylor?" Sage rested her head against her brother's shoulder.

"I think I do," he said. "He's not a stranger, you know. He looks like you."

"Except he's skinny."

"So are you, dumbbell."

"Do you suppose he likes me?" Sage asked. "Even though I've caused him all this trouble?"

Tobias laughed and took her hand. "Probably he does," he said, kissing her fingers.

After Sage was released from the hospital, Tobias sat in the rented van with her on the drive to Emmy's apartment, where she was going to stay to recover. She lay in the backseat under comforters, her head on Tobias's lap, John Taylor driving, Jacob sitting in the passenger seat next to him.

"Would you have known me on a crowded street even though you'd never seen me?" Sage asked her father once.

"What do you think?" he replied.

"I think yes," she said.

Chapter Nineteen

I changed rooms when I came back to this university for the spring semester, changed dormitories, started again as a freshman. My new room is larger and brighter, overlooking the halting beginnings of spring in the park outside—a cluster of trees, banks of budding yellow daffodils.

It's gloriously sunny today, though cold for the start of April, and I'm packing up my books for an eight-o'clock Spanish class. My roommate is sleeping. She is new here this semester, new to America, a homesick young woman from Malaysia who is studying medicine. We will not be close friends, but I'm glad to have her here.

She has told me she doesn't like American women because they're pushy, but she likes me, she says, because I'm a little mouse. I told her what happened to me last semester, how I thought I was being followed by Steven Carney, how I locked myself in my room for three weeks without eating or drinking and finally lost consciousness and spent a month in the hospital. I told her that my mother had died and that she was a doctor.

Last Tuesday, when I came into the room from a history class, she was leaning over my desk looking at the three framed pictures of my family there: Mama and me in the back garden; all of us children when we were little, standing on the front steps in our Easter clothes; and a picture taken at Christmas in front of the house on Moran Street, just after it was sold to a family from Kansas City. My father and me and Maggie and Emmy and Jacob and Caroline and Tobias. Winona took the picture.

Good-bye, Moran Street, I have written on the back.

"Keep still," Winona is saying. "Smile, John. Don't look so glum."

"He's not glum," Jacob says.

John Taylor is holding Maggie, who is pulling on

his ear. I stand next to him, my hands in the pockets of my ski jacket.

"Move in a little closer here," my father says to me, and I do so but not too close—after all, we are all thinking the same thing even though we don't say it out loud: What would Mama say to see us here in her house, finally sold, with John Jefferson Taylor.

My father must have thought that too, because he doesn't stay in the house with us.

"Louisa might be aggravated to have me spend the night," is what he said.

Emmy said Mama would be glad to know that he was taking charge, especially of me. She worried about me. I know that. And now he's here, and it feels as if he'd been here always, all my life.

"Did you ever think to call us?" Caroline asks him, still unforgiving.

"Did you ever try to see us?" Emmy asks.

"I did," John Taylor says. "I talked to your mother. But you know how your mother was. She said no, absolutely. No chance."

"Emmy says Mama was so mad because she still loved you," Tobias tells him.

"Could be we loved each other always," my father answers.

He puts his arm around my shoulder and kisses my cheek. I like the smoky smell of him, his blue-black hands, large for a small man, and graceful.

"*You look* like your father," my roommate tells me.

"I know," I say. "I'm the only child who does."

He calls me from New York often, twice a week at least, sometimes more.

"How're you doing?" he'll ask. The question is not casual.

I answer honestly. "Better," I say. This is true almost any day I'm asked. Better than the day before.

I almost died.

"Severe dehydration, with complications," the doctors at the hospital said.

Terror was more exact.

Even now, on my way to class, I know my Fear List is in place in the second drawer of my dresser in my new dormitory room.

"Things change," my father told me at Christmas. "But not completely. After all, who would want to turn into someone else?"

I check the clock beside my bed, call Emmy in Boston and Jacob in St. Louis, and put a message on my father's voice mail. Tobias calls me every morning at seven before he goes to his new coaching job.

At eight, I leave for Spanish class, running down the front stairs of the dormitory, out the door into the pure cold morning, into the crowds of students moving toward their classes. Occasionally on mornings like this, cold, the air too thin for proper breathing, I see Steven Carney walking with a group, a little taller than the rest of them, or standing across the street with his back to me, or leaning over a water fountain in the science building.

I think I see him, but when I look again, look carefully, take the whole of him into account, it is not Steven Carney at all. Only a memory of someone missing, a sudden hunger, a silver glimmer of imagination reflected on a stranger in a crowd.